KER DUKEY

IT FEELS GOOD TO SIN.

~~lust~~

pride

wrath

envy

greed

gluttony

sloth

Lust

ISBN: 9781794529120

Cover Design: All By Design
Photo: Adobe Stock
Editor: Word Nerd Editing
Proofread: Kim BookJunkie
Formatting: Champagne Book Design

For my darKER Souls

My sinners who want that

neck biting, hair pulling, skin slapping, ass spanking, back scratching, angry kinda sex.

Life is for living.

So live.

Wild, dirty, and free to sin.

PREFACE

the elite seven

Since 1942, The Elite Seven Society has created and guided influential leaders, molding the country into something better. This society was birthed by Malcom Benedict II, who wanted more for Americans. More wealth. More influence. More power. Some leaders have the skills, but not the influence, and that simply wasn't fair according to Mr. Benedict. He invested his own money and time to construct a society that bred the best of the best, year after year.

But to be the best, you must be ruthless.

Good leaders make sacrifices. Sometimes the sacrifices are hard, but the rewards are plentiful. Mr. Benedict made sure to indulge these leaders with their utmost desires. A devout Catholic himself, he designed a society that rewarded his leaders with the sins that were frowned upon. If they were giving up love and happiness and joy for the betterment of the country, they deserved something in its stead.

Pride, Envy, Wrath, Sloth, Greed, Gluttony, and Lust.

Choosing leaders for this society takes intense focus. Only seven are to be selected, and the investment and time are showered upon the new seven chosen every four years. The university's acting dean behaves as a liaison for the society, bringing the applicants to the predecessors so the selection may begin. The society members going out will bring forth a candidate the society votes on and approves.

After they are chosen, the initiates are given a token and an invitation to initiation. The initiation tests their character and ability to do what's right for the betterment of the society. Once the initiates pass their test, they are discreetly branded with the mark of the society and groomed through challenges during the course of their elite education to breed them into the influential people they were meant to be.

Once in The Elite Seven, there is no getting out. The money and power are their reward. Should they choose to stray or break the rules, the society strips them of everything. Anything they once had will be removed. Opportunities will never arise. They will no longer have the support of the society. To this day, there have been no known occurrences of anyone from the society having to be banished. Every young man and woman aspires to be a part of the elite group whispered about amongst the privileged. Anyone who is anyone knows of the group and secretly hopes their son or daughter is selected, for good fortune is showered on the family for decades to come.

These violent delights have violent ends ~ William Shakespeare.

—Romeo and Juliet.

UINCENDUM NATUS

LUST

PROLOGUE

Rhett
20:15

The clock on my dashboard mocks me. Late is an understatement.

Punishing the throttle, I will my tires to stick to the wet road as the storm rattles the sky above me. Like it's releasing the fucking Kraken.

I love living in New Orleans but the weather in hurricane season is a bipolar bitch. Soaking rain with high winds that could blow the skin off a gator one minute, hotter than Satan's asshole the next.

My wipers battle to give me visual as I pass the sign telling me half a mile to my turn off.

Static white noise crackles through the radio, breaking up the vocals of Post Malone's new track, and smacking the thing doesn't seem to fix the problem.

This night has turned to shit fast, and it's only going to get worse when my mother finds out how late I was picking up my kid brother.

Groaning at the time ticking by, I try to focus, my speed eating up the pavement.

Blue and red lights flash through the smog of the rain in front of me, and I slow the car to a roll before I can even reach the exit I need to take.

Perfect.

Slamming my hands on the steering wheel, I squint through the rivulets of water pouring all around.

Orange cones block the road, forcing me to idle the car.

The rain punishes the windshield, blurring my sight, making it almost impossible to make out what's going on outside.

Fuck.

Like I need this shit.

All I can think about is Robbie waiting outside his Karate class alone, soaking wet and no doubt starving.

I'm a shit big brother, selfish. The guilt is building, and whatever the fuck's happened here is bad. I'm not going to get moving anytime soon.

Ignoring the constant beeping of my cell phone with texts from our anxious mother, I open a message from my best friend asking me to bail on the party tonight and go dragging with him instead.

He's got a death wish to risk drag racing in this weather. Hard pass.

I shoot him a message back, telling him to come to the party for a few hours first, then chuck my cell in the passenger seat.

I'll get him drunk tonight—which is all too fucking easy with him—and take his keys away. No racing and dying tonight.

I roll down the window and try to flag down one of the officers laying out cones to prevent traffic from coming through on the other side.

"Sir, I really need to get through here," I call out, waving my arm in an attempt to get his attention.

Thunder rumbles from above, followed by a lightening show dancing in the clouds.

This storm wasn't supposed to hit until tomorrow.

Rain instantly begins pouring in through the open window, soaking me and the leather interior of my new dodge charger. The selfish prick I am, it irritates me I'm even in this situation.

I should be getting ready for the house party on the other side of town.

Our dad was supposed to pick Robbie up, but once again, he had to work late. It wouldn't be that bad if his office weren't five blocks over.

Dick.

Most boys admired their father, but not me. Mine was a pretentious prick who hated that I chose to pursue a football scholarship instead of taking his money and following him into the world of finance.

He made it no secret that Robbie was his favourite kid, and hell, I didn't blame him. Just because we're related, there are no rules that say we can't clash—and clash we do.

An officer approaches my window wearing plastic overalls that do nothing to prevent the fierce winds from blowing the rain sideways into his face. Poor bastard.

"You'll need to turn around, sir," he instructs, and irritation grinds my bones.

I can practically see the building through the gathering of magnolia trees lining the opposite side of the road.

Inhaling a frustrated breath, I look to the grass border on my side, then nod to the officer. "Fine"

I watch him walk away in my wing mirror, making his way to a car pulling up behind me, no doubt giving them the same instructions to turn around.

Fuck it. I'll have to jog the rest of the way and get wet.

Pulling my car over to the side of the road, I jump out and immediately regret my choice of not wearing a coat today. My boots slap on the asphalt that's becoming more like a river than a road.

The officer jogs back toward me, hurried and pissed off, pointing at my car.

"You can't leave your car there," he shouts, shaking his head.

I look past him to an ambulance stopping by two police cars parked at an odd angle in the road. Squinting my eyes, I make out a truck just beyond them. Looks like it collided with a tree.

I can only see the back end and don't recognize the licence plate, thank fuck.

"I just need to run over and pick my brother up from his karate class. I'm late, and he's only twelve, sir," I say, trying to appeal to his humanity.

Rain makes it hard to speak. It's pouring over me, drenching my clothes. Without a jacket on, my shirt becomes a second skin, slick and stuck to me like glue. My jeans become heavy, and a frigid whisper skitters up my spine as Mother Nature breathes down my neck.

I hate the sploshing of my boots as I take a step forward, pushing a hand through my hair to remove it from my eyes.

Leaves rip from the trees and dance to the tune of the wind picking up speed.

The officer has gone silent. He looks through the trees to where I gesture, then back to the sight of the incident.

Sirens blast through the quiet night, and my eyes scan the road as a fire engine approaches.

I nod over to the accident. "That bad, huh?" I wince, folding my arms to ward off some of the chill cutting through me.

"What's your brother's name?" he asks, pulling me from being a nosey bastard trying to get a look around him at the damage.

Seeing a guy sitting in the back of one of the cop cars wrapped in a blanket, I ask, "That the driver? He okay?"

"What's your brother's name, son." He turns his head to hear me better, ignoring my question.

Shit. *Robbie* has to be freaking out. He's a sensitive kid and it's getting dark. I really need to go.

"Robbie, and he's going to be really worried. He was expecting my mother an hour ago," I confess, my shoulders jerking with guilt.

I'm a piece of shit. My mother asked me to go get him because she was caught up with something and Dad dropped the *working late* shit on her.

She made me promise not to forget or be late, and I was too busy getting head from the captain of the cheerleader squad. Such an asshole.

I'd been trying to get her on my list since I started at

that school, and she'd held out—until today. She's a bad bitch too. Deep throats like a pro.

Filthy and fucking thirsty for dick, she exceeded all my expectations.

"And you said he's eleven?" the officer continues, bringing me back from the memory of her lips around me.

"Twelve," I correct with a frustrated grunt.

Dude, I don't have time for this. Fuck, I hope he's not thinking we neglected him or some shit. Mom's going to have my balls for this.

"You have a picture of him?"

"What, why?"

What the hell? Why the fuck would he want a picture?

Firefighters pour onto the scene, their voices are raised to be heard over the torrent making their job twice as hard.

I strain to listen, and a rock forms in my gut at their words.

"He's pinned from the chest down. As soon as we separate the truck, he's going to drop. We need to secure his body."

Damn, that sounds brutal.

"I need to go. I promise I'll be quick," I shout to the officer as I take off jogging. He calls out to me, but I've wasted enough time.

Going around the fire truck, I cut through the trees. The wind howls, tossing the branches around violently. They whip me across the face, scraping holes into my flesh. My feet sink into the ground with each determined step, submerging me in more than one puddle, flooding my boots.

LUST

By the time I make it through the brush, I'm a mess. Mud cakes my boots and jeans, and I may as well not be wearing a shirt. My dark hair flops over my eyes, blinding me.

Mom's going to owe me for this shit.

I cross the street, and my stomach knots when I don't see Robbie's silhouette under the lamppost where he's supposed to wait.

Shit.

Scanning the parking lot, I look for any sheltered areas he might have taken refuge, but there's nowhere he could be.

Jogging over to the building, I grab the handle on the door and give it a tug, but it's locked and there are no lights coming from inside.

Mom had warned me this was the last class of the night and they lock the building up so Robbie would be outside with no way of getting back in.

I'm a cunt.

There's a pounding in my chest—a vibrating, nervous energy trying to rip from under my skin with each passing second he's not materialising in front of me.

Where are you?

The sky darkens with each fleeting breath I take, my body jolting with the thunder as it rips through the night.

Unease settles in my chest, and panic races up my throat as I call out for him.

"Robbie!" I shout, water spraying from my lips.

Nothing.

"Robbie," I try again, my tone more urgent. I pat down my pockets for my cell, but already know I left it in the car. Fuck. Fuck.

The lights from the emergency vehicles taunt me through the trees, then someone emerging through the same brush I just came from catches my eye and I take off in their direction.

I come to a slow walk when I see the silhouette is too large to be Robbie.

It's the officer from before.

What the hell?

My car's not even in anyone's way, and finding my brother is more important. Let the jerk give me a ticket.

"What's your name, son?" he asks, coming to a stop in front of me.

"Rhett. Rhett Masters, why?" I bark, anger and fear eating away at me.

He looks around me to the building where Robbie should be, then back to me.

"He's not here," I tell him before he gets suspicious that I was making shit up.

Where are you, Robbie?

"Ok, I need you to listen to me and prepare yourself for what I'm going to tell you." His eyes hold mine with an intensity that makes every hair on my body rise.

Thud.

My head swims, and there's this knowledge taking over my mind I can't possibly predict, but my head turns to the emergency chaos happening through the trees and I stagger backwards.

Robbie.

"Wait. Wait, no, no." I shake my head, holding out my arm to him. I'm not prepared to hear what I know he's going to tell me.

I just fucking know he's going to say something bad.

LUST

The darkness of the impending night wraps its angry fist around my throat and begins to squeeze.

"The accident…a truck swerved off the road and hit a boy."

Stop.

Don't fucking say it.

"We believe him to be around eleven or twelve years old."

Shut up. I can't hear this.

"He's wearing a Karate Gi."

Thud. Thud. Thud.

Robbie.

Thick fog begins stirring inside my mind, making me woozy. My stomach clenches, and I dry heave.

It's not Robbie. This isn't real.

No.

No fucking way.

I try to tell my mind it's not factual, but I feel the truth constricting my heart.

Robbie tried to walk because I left him here and now he's pinned by a truck to a tree.

"He didn't make it," the officer says, placing a hand on my shoulder. "I'm sorry, son."

No.

My head shakes back and forth manically, and I bat his hand off me.

"He died on impact. He wouldn't have felt a thing."

Take that back.

It's not Robbie.

"Can you come with me? We need to contact your parents." He makes a move with his hand, but I step away.

No.

Shut the fuck up. Stop touching me.

My legs steady themselves, becoming solid once more beneath me instead of jelly, and I run.

Before I even realize it, I've cleared the trees and I'm at the truck.

Thud... Thud....

"Whoa, what the hell? Move away now," someone barks, but my knees fail me.

"Robbie," I yell, tears clogging my throat and acid burning in my chest.

It's then I see it—his backpack peeking up just over the bumper—his brown hair soaked to his head that's slumped to the side.

Robbie. My baby brother...

Arms and hands grab at me, but I pull away, stumbling back and falling on my ass to the muddy ground beneath me. My heart is going to burst through my chest, tears burn my eyes, and vomit chases my soul, vacating my body.

"Get him away," voices shout, but everything is threatening to fade out.

Mother Nature tears the sky apart above, mourning along with me for what I've lost.

My arms reach out, grasping air. "Robbie," I choke.

It's my fault.

It's my fucking fault.

ONE

Nothing is real.

Nothing feels solid anymore.

The casket is too small.

This shouldn't be happening.

"In the Arms of the Angels" croons through the cemetery from invisible speakers, and the air feels toxic.

Like I'm breathing in poison and it's constricting my lungs, choking me. I wish it would crawl up my throat and strangle me so I don't have to be here to feel this mourning.

My father sits, controlled and composed next to me, but his knuckles are white as he squeezes his gloves in his palm. Dark shades frame his face, hiding his sorrow behind them.

Flower arrangements formed into words mock me

from the space separating us from his casket.

Son.

Brother.

I don't even recognize half the people here. Sobs and sniffles sound all around me, and I want to block them out—claw at the mud to fill my own ears so I don't have to witness their pain. Hear their grief.

It's all too fucking much.

It's all because of me.

When the casket begins to lower into the ground, a sound like I've never heard before rips from my mother's lips, shattering the air and causing every hair follicle on my body to rise.

If death had a sound, it would be the broken wails of my mother. She's dying, her broken heart ripping her to shreds for all to witness.

A chill races over my body, dampening my skin in a sheen of frost.

"No, no, no! Not my baby! Please! I'm sorry! I'm so sorry Robbie…" she howls, grief wrapping her in its tormenting grip and squeezing the air from her lungs.

Chest pains signal the cracking of my own ribcage as my heart spills free at her feet.

This is my fault.

I'm sorry, Mom.

The sky darkens as grey clouds roll in as If summoned by her pain. Rain pelts down, throwing my mind back to that night.

"He didn't make it, son."

Tears burn my eyes as I get to my feet and reach out for my mother, but she slaps my hands away, and any soul left inside me dissipates.

LUST

"Don't touch me," she chokes out. "I can't look at you."

I stumble away from her, ignoring the voices of my best friend and family members as they try to console me.

My feet move, and before I even realize it, I'm running.

Echoes of people shouting at me fade into the distance as rain pours over their words.

My legs burn, carrying me in the direction of the main road.

I don't know how long I'm pounding the asphalt, but my lungs scream for relief. My boots have torn my feet to shreds, and the pain washes out the reality of why I'm running.

Focusing on the burn of my limbs, I will the images of my dead brother to vacate my mind.

The casket lowering into a dirt hole.

I want to feel numb, please, God.

The rhythm of my heart is erratic and labored by the time I reach the parking lot of where Robbie took Karate.

I don't know why I'm here or how long it took me to get here, but the day is turning to night and the rain is dousing me in its memory of his death.

I'm choking on the downpour coating my lips as I gasp at the air to cool the lava in my lungs.

Everything feels suspended in time, like slow motion. My steps become heavy and sluggish as I approach the trees and push through the branches, twigs snapping underfoot.

When I clear the treeline, my body solidifies.

The tree is still there. It looks unmarked.

Tall and flourishing like nothing happened.

My brother's life ended, and the world keeps turning, life goes on.

Water cascades down all around me just like that night, and my mind spins and churns. But it's not just rain staining cheeks. Sobs wreck and ravage me, buckling my knees and bringing me to the ground.

Everything fucking hurts. My heart wants to flee, but as punishment for what I've done, it can't escape. It's trapped inside me to suffer in agony.

"Rhett?"

"Rhett?"

I hear my name, but I can't tell what's real and what's not anymore.

My features pinch in confusion when lights flash and a car pulls up behind me.

The headlights illuminate the scene, lighting up everything I want kept in the dark.

"Robbie." I heave his name, my stomach roiling, and body losing all ability to hold me upright. The darkness opens its arms to me, and I fall to meet it.

TWO

One Month Later…

Alcohol and coke burns in my bloodstream, giving me a false sense of courage.

Cheers ring out from the partygoers below, and the pool blurs my eyesight.

Holding up the bottle of Jack Daniels I have a brief recollection of being handed by my best friend, Baxter Goddard, aka God, I shout, "One!"

God, from the pool below, shouts back, "Two!"

The crowd continues the count, calling out, "Three!"

I down the contents of the bottle and take a running leap off the roof.

"Ohhh shit," rings out from below, but it's too late. The buzz of liquor hums through my veins, air whooshes past me in a flash, and then I'm hitting water, the cold liquid consuming me on entry.

A jolt sparks up my ankle, zapping a sharp stab of pain through my foot, and then everyone is cheering as I break the surface. Opening my eyes I float in the shallow end of the water.

"Oh fuck! There's blood," someone cries out, and next thing I know, I'm being dragged out of the pool by God.

My blood? I think to myself, but the reality of what's happening doesn't penetrate my drunken haze.

"Fuck! Call an ambulance!"

Laughter cackles from me, rattling my entire body.

I don't feel human right now.

Am I losing my mind?

A burly white dude with a skinhead and tattoos up his neck kneels in front of me and rubs his chin. "That's pretty grim, man. The bone pierced through the skin."

"You in any pain?" God asks, and I snort, pushing at him playfully.

"My brother's killer was given a fucking fine. I'm numb," I tell him honestly, and then the laughter turns to sorrow, and I can't stop the tears and desperate hands tugging at my sanity.

Someone's knocking on the door to the recesses of my mind, and it's the old me, begging me to let him take back the wheel.

Fuck him.

Slouching back, I close my eyes to shut out all the faces looking down on me.

A throb begins to pound behind my eyelids, and everything swirls around inside me like a tornado, dragging me under into the calm of the storm.

LUST

It's too quiet.

Eerie.

I'm in the middle of the road. The asphalt is wet, but it's not raining.

"Rhett."

My name is whispered on the gentle breeze rustling through the trees, and my breath hitches.

"Where are you, Rhett?"

My heart rate is elevated, pounding through my chest, beating through the skin.

Placing a hand there, I search the treeline for someone…for him.

"Don't forget about me, Rhett."

"Robbie!" I shout.

"I'm here."

My entire frame jolts, and I brush at my ear, certain the whisper echoed there.

My eyes spring open, and I'm propelled into consciousness.

A dull yellow glow lights the room bringing it into view.

The shadows shift and move until a figure steps out from them, and I exhale an unsteady breath.

Emotion, heavy and weighted, pushes down on my chest, and tears burn my eyes.

My mother comes to stand at the base of the hospital bed I appear to be in.

"Mom?" I croak.

My mouth feels like it's been left open for a week and

moths have taken up residence.

"Do you know how terrifying it is to get a call informing me my son is in the hospital?" she says, shaking her head, exhausted.

Her brown curly hair matches my own, messy and chaotic, and full lips tug down her pretty features. Red-rimmed eyes pin me to the spot, and guilt cloaks my body like a blanket.

"I'm sorry," I say.

"So am I, Rhett. I can't stick around and watch you self-destruct. It hurts too much. I've lost too much. Suffered more than…" she chokes, but there's a resolve in her tone that leaves a pit in my stomach.

My mouth opens, but words fail me.

Her hand comes to rest on my leg, and it's then I notice my other leg is suspended in the air, hanging in a sling with a cast from my shin to my toes.

"You snapped the bone. Ruined your football career before it even took off."

She swipes at a stray tear and sniffs, shaking her head again.

"Your grades are slipping, and the school is worried about you graduating."

"I don't care about any of that shit anymore," I tell her honestly.

Her features transform from sorrow to anger, and she rounds the bed, coming to stop right next to my head.

"You better start caring. You lived, Rhett. You didn't die that night, Robbie did, and I'll be damned if I'm going to watch you piss your life away in his memory. You owe him more than that—more than this!" She punctuates each word with a pointed finger to my chest.

Guilt, rooted all the way to my bone marrow, infects me. It's like an illness inside me I can't recover from.

"That son of a bitch who killed him got a fine—a fucking fine! He was over the limit!" I weep, tears brimming and falling from my eyes. I know it's selfish of me to put all my anger and pain on her. She must feel a million times worse than I do.

I hate it. I hate this. I hate him. I hate myself.

Closing her eyes, she hugs her arms around her waist like she needs to hold herself together or she'll crumble to dust.

"The system is full of injustices. Instead of becoming part of the problem, become part of the solution," she snaps. "Make your life count for something."

Without another word, she leaves the room.

Our house.

Our town.

She leaves me.

THREE

2 months later…

Order pizza. Working late. Dad.

I snort at the note left on the fridge. It's the same one that gets reposted at least four nights a week.

He's hardly ever home, and that suits me just fine. I swipe the twenty he left and stuff it in my pocket.

He's tightened my allowance these days and took my credit card as punishment for renting out an entire hotel for my friends and me after our prom.

It was worth it. If I can live in the illusion of who I used to be before Robbie's death, it helps me forget—if only for a moment. I long for those moments where I get a sliver of reprieve from the anger, the guilt, the goddamn sorrow.

Locking the front door behind me, I jog down the street, keeping my steps light.

LUST

God meets me at the bottom of my road with a gas can and tube in his hand, a cocky smirk on his face.

"I ain't doing the sucking," he informs me, handing me the instruments for tonight's activity.

"You always suck," I gest, taking the jab to the arm he gives me.

His brown, almond-shaped eyes clash with mine, a mischievous gleam shining through.

Most people who don't know us assume we're related with our similar looks and brotherly bond.

We're both tall and athletic, dark hair and eyes, full lips and chiseled jawlines.

We're a dynamic duo.

"Why can't we just go to the gas station and fill it up?" he moans, looking up and down the street to make sure no one is around to see us syphoning gas from my neighbors' cars.

"Because we don't want to be on any video surveillance that can be used as evidence," I tell him again. We've already been over this a few times.

Losing my scholarship was crushing once it really sank in.

My mom's parting words at the hospital after my stupid accident really struck a cord with me, and since she's been gone, my old man's been a thorn in my fucking side.

Using money for school as a tool to keep me in line.

Fuck him.

He's been flaunting his ass all over town, making a mockery of his marriage and my mom.

I fucking hate him and can't wait to be out from under him.

"You sure you want to do this? I can speak to my dad

for you." God pulls out his cell phone. "This could be a hoax," he grumbles.

"Or a test," I remind him.

Rumor has it someone has proof that a secret society, The Elite, is in fact a real thing.

To most, it's an urban legend, whispered about amongst high schoolers, but to those of us who know it exists know becoming a member brings opportunity, belonging, wealth, knowledge, and status.

God's father, Baxter Samuel Goddard IV, or Four, as his friends call him, bears the mark of The Elite in form of a tattoo, yet he's yet to confirm he's in fact a member to his own son.

That's how secret and elite this society is. However, I fucking know it's true.

When I was twelve and staying over at God's, one of God's favourite pastimes was daring me to do shit. This one night, he had dared me to sneak into his father's office and replace the "good" bourbon his father kept in there with cheap stuff he paid some hobo to buy for him in town. God's always had issues with his father, like I said; we're cut from the same cloth.

I was just about to exit Four's office after completing the dare, when I heard his heavy footfalls approach. I had to find a place to hide. Lucky for me, Four needed a big office to fit his huge ego.

6 years ago

I dart across the room my head swivelling in all directions until I notice a slither of space down by the couch along the back wall.

LUST

The door opens and my eyes scan his movements. I can see him clearly, his cell glued to his ear.

My eyes track him as he goes to the huge self-portrait of himself positioned in the centre of the main wall.

The artist who created it had missed out a few of Four's chins but captured the greed always alight in his eyes.

When he opens the frame like a door it causes my mouth to pop open, a safe is displayed behind it built into the wall.

That's freaking cool.

Punching in numbers it beeps and releases the safe door.

Reaching inside he pulls out a book of some kind; it has an emblem of a skull covering the front with words that I can't make out from this distance. With his cell to his ear he frowns and then speaks down the line.

"With her inheriting all his businesses it's even more imperative that we recruit her into The Elite."

Taking a few heavy breaths he shakes his head slightly before continuing.

"That was college. She's made a life for herself since then, maybe we give her a little incentive. I want her name in this book." He grunts, plonking the book down on his desk and straining his ass into the seat before grabbing a handful of candy from a bowl on his desk, shovelling them into his mouth like he's never going to get a meal again.

"I'm leaving this to you, get it done." He almost chokes through the sugar in his mouth before chucking the phone down.

Inquisitive by nature my hands become jittery with a need to see this book. It looks like something you'd see in a Jumanji movie, a treasure of some kind.

Picking up a pen, he flicks through the pages until he finds what he's looking for and strokes his wrist over the surface, adding ink to the paper.

Closing the book he strains to stand back up and groans when his knees click under the pressure of his weight. I move further back until I'm flush with the wall. He locks the book back away and waddles past the couch I'm hidden next to and disappears out the room.

Present.

It was two years later when I finally got to see the book.

God's parents were away on business and my best friend had a bad habit of needing to chase adrenaline highs. Stealing his father's brand new Bugatti Veyron would give him just that.

The car cost a cool two million so the keys were kept in Four's office safe.

Little did I know God had worked out the combination a year earlier.

There was a lot of fortune in that safe, but my curiosity was on one thing. That book. *"What the fuck you want to look at a book for?"* God snorted. I remember his nonchalant shrug as if it was yesterday when I told him to give me a few minutes with it.

4 Years earlier.

"Whatever, just hurry up, Jasmine and Angela are waiting for us." He grins.

Reaching inside the safe I pull out the book.

It looks thicker since the last time I saw it, but that could just be because I'm seeing it up close.

It's heavy, weighted by the leather and metal woven into the front cover.

A skull wearing a crown is raised from the surface, I run my fingers over the detail feeling like I've found something otherworldly. Secret. Precious.

Roman numerals adding up to seven sit beneath the skull and words written in a language I can't read are scrawled beneath them.

UNICENDUM NATUS

Opening the book the first page makes my heart stampede.

Members of

THE ELITE SEVEN SOCIETY.

Pages and pages of businesses and familiar names fill the paper.

My hands shake when I come to a page with my last name written at the top.

MASTERS

A list of our family tree written beneath and a log of all businesses owned by family members.

How can a society have so much information on everyone?

My stomach bottoms out when my eyes read over a declined stamp in big red letters next to each person printed there.

Declined from what?

"Rhett, let's go man, we got rubber to burn." God barks at me and snatches the book from my grasp stuffing it back into the safe.

Present.

My name wasn't in there. I only pray my name has been added now and an acceptance stamp gets printed next to it. I've never seen the book since.

When Four returned from his trip he was told of God's antics, driving through the town in a car owned by only a few men in the entire world.

It was hard to deny we stole the car for a joy ride.

Four upped his security system and we've been locked out ever since.

I'm convinced God's name will show up on that list, and I want to be on it with him.

Since losing my potential football career, I've become obsessed with The Elite. But there is little information out there about them. All we really know is only seven members are initiated each year, and those members are to be the best of the best—members who can become an asset to society—and this mission tonight is to solidify my name amongst those seven.

A rumor surfaced that a document of proof that The Elite exists is going to be leaked to the local press. A manila envelope containing damning details has been posted today to the press office.

Most people have rolled their eyes at this gossip, but I think it's a test.

The Elite is testing new potential recruits to see if anyone will try to retrieve the letter.

I'm going to do one better.

I suck the pipe and spit out the gas as it fills my mouth. Sticking the pipe in the can, I grin as it fills.

Sorry, Mrs. Barnes. We need the gas more.

I move from her white sedan to the other neighbor's truck. It only takes the two before the can is filled to the brim.

"That was gross." I spit a few times to clear the residue from my gums.

Jogging down the road to God's car, a blood-red Ferrari Pininfarina Sergio—flashy son of a bitch, we jump in and drive in silence along the back roads to keep off the radar of cameras or law enforcement.

I get him to drop me off a couple blocks down from the sorting office.

All mail ends up here, ready to be delivered, and working times are four a.m. to ten p.m., so the building will be empty.

"You sure you don't want me to come with?" God asks, pulling the car to the side of the road next to an old abandoned factory building.

"Nah. Just meet me back at my house and we can hit up Winter's party. Get an alibi for the night."

"Sounds good. Be careful."

Slipping behind the structures, I stick to the shadows, making sure the hood of my jacket covers most of my face in case there are cameras on any of the buildings.

When I reach the sorting office, I do a lap around the block. It's past eleven, so the place should be empty, but double checking puts my mind at ease. No lights are on inside, and no cars litter the parking lot.

Unscrewing the cap on the gas can, I begin pouring a barrier around the building. Once I've done a full circle, I stuff a rag in the end of the bottle, light it, and send it hurtling through one of the windows.

A whooshing sounds, and then the smell hits my nostrils. It's not long before a crackling of flames licks up the windows.

I light the trail outside the building, and within minutes, the entire place goes up like kindling.

Smiling, I make a run for it, ignoring the dull ache

shooting up the side of my leg from my old foot injury.

I make it four blocks, then my stomach bottoms out.

Blue lights flash and a cop car pulls over.

Fuck.

FOUR

Staring at my old man, I focus on his lips moving, but I stopped listening to him once he said he was relaying my mom's message because she didn't want to see me to tell me herself.

"Are you listening to me?" he barks, and I've honestly never felt this disconnected, lost. I need him to fuck off so I can get out of here and escape in liquor and women.

"Sorry I missed that last part." I rub a hand over my face before crossing my arms over my chest.

Rolling his eyes, he pinches the bridge of his nose and exhales an exasperated breath.

"Terms of your enrollment is you'll see a guidance counselor once a week."

"Why?"

"Because you've been acting out since your brother's

death, breaking bones and burning down buildings!" he shouts.

Slouching back on the couch, I shrug a shoulder.

"There was no proof I started that fire. No charges were brought against me."

"Yet," he corrects. "You're lucky you're best friends with a Goddard."

Getting to my feet, I pull on my jacket and swipe my keys from the table.

"Until then, I'm innocent."

"Where do you think you're going?" he snaps. I hate the look in his eyes: disdain and regret. It wouldn't be so bad if his eyes weren't a reflection of my own.

"Out. Going to celebrate getting into college." I smile tightly.

Snatching my keys from my hand, he chucks them back on the table and walks around me, stating, "By the skin of your teeth and the graces of your family ties—that's what got you into college. There's nothing worth celebrating about that."

The ribbon keeping my temper together fragments and tugs away, until it completely unravels. "Fuck you," I growl.

He turns sharp, his dark eyes penetrating mine. Marching toward me, he stops a foot away. His chest is puffed out and shoulders are back, but there's wariness in his approach that wasn't there before this moment.

Our height is equal these days. I'm topping just over six-foot, and my frame is slightly slimmer than his due to all the running for football, but I'm packing all muscle. If it came down to it and he threw a punch, I know I could take it and deliver one back just as powerful.

"Tread carefully, Rhett. I could take all this away just as quick as it was given."

His threat is menacing and hits me harder than a punch ever could.

Fuck him.

I'll walk to God's and we can party there.

It wasn't the plan for me and God to end up at the same college, but it's a fucking bonus worth celebrating nonetheless.

FIVE

Loud drumming pounds all around me. The room is filled with bodies jumping up and down to the beat. Everyone is shouting, throwing themselves into each other like idiots. I have no fucking clue how I ended up here.

Walls plastered with posters close in on me, and red cups litter the holey couch I'm sitting on.

Some female is gyrating on my lap, making my cock jump in my pants while she chants along to some lyrics being yelled into a mic.

I can barely make out God across the room joining in with the weird jumping around shit. We're not used to or interested in this type of music, yet he's acting like he is.

This is typical of God. He has more money than sense and a cocksure attitude that makes most normal people quake. That's his dad in him—the "I rule the world" attitude.

Coming to a party like this is entertaining to him. His family is no doubt richer than all these peoples' families combined, and slumming it with the basic folk amuses him. He has a sick sense of humor.

A voice growls into a mic, and the atmosphere spikes. Beer rains down on us as drinks are sloshed around.

The music cuts off, and someone's voice echoes through the room.

"Thanks for coming out to support us tonight. Make sure you buy a CD before you leave. Only five dollars."

Where the fuck are we?

"You want to come back to my house?" the girl on my lap asks in a sexy, deep southern drawl.

Scanning my eyes over her, I take note of a pixie haircut with a rainbow of color through it.

Nose and lip piercings draw my attention, and I grin down at her.

"What else you got pierced?"

Her giggle is carefree and light.

"You'll have to come find out."

Slipping off my lap, she takes my hand, helping me to my feet and dragging me though the crowd.

I look over to see God disappearing through a side door with two women. Never simple with him. Everything he does is in excess.

"Where do you live?" I wrap an arm around the chick's shoulder and lean down to nibble her earlobe.

We exit the room into a fresh breeze and more bodies partying in the streets.

"Just there," she breathes, leaning into my lips. It's

then I realize we were in someone's garage a few houses down from where this chick lives.

I don't recognize this part of town, or how the fuck we got here, but that's not unusual when you're friends with God. It's like he finds the seediest shitholes just to spite his father.

We topple through her front door, and she tosses a set of keys down before turning around to face me. She walks backwards, pulling me with her.

"You want a drink?"

Fuck yes.

"What you got?"

She bites her lips, pondering my question, then pushes me into a living room.

"Go make yourself comfortable. I'll get us something."

A large orange couch dominates the room, calling me to it. I shrug off my jacket and collapse down, laying my full length across the cushions. It's itchy as shit, but I'm lacking the drive to move just yet.

The chick appears upside down above me a few seconds later, and I'm grateful I didn't close my eyes. Robbie waits for me there, and its too painful.

"Vodka?" She grins, holding out a glass for me.

Shifting into a sitting position, I take the glass and down the contents, savoring the chase of fire down my throat.

"Whoa, slow down, stud." She takes the empty glass and places it on the coffee table before sliding herself onto my lap.

She's a petite little thing, wearing a pair of tiny jean shorts and a band tee.

Her small tits don't offer even a handful, but the confidence dripping off her is hella sexy.

My cock stirs, and I try to blank out the voice whispering from the dark corners of my mind.

"Where were you, Rhett?"

When she notices my distracted state, she goes for my belt buckle, but I place a hand over hers, stopping her and moving her from my lap.

Large green eyes expand and her smile falters as I chip away at that confidence.

"Everything okay?" she asks, her voice meek. It makes me feel like a douchebag causing her to question herself.

"Yeah, everything's real good. I just want to look at you." I slide my hands beneath her top and draw it up over her body, tugging it over her head.

Pale skin decorated with color expands down her chest, ending at her tiny pink nipples that peak into little pebbles. Leaning up, I take one in my mouth, swirling my tongue over the bud, then sucking her entire tit into my mouth before releasing it with a loud pop.

I jerk open the buttons of her jean shorts and yank them down her legs.

She's not wearing underwear and has a small patch of hair she colored pink.

What the fuck?

She grins at me. "Never had pink pussy before?"

A real laugh barks out of me, and I fall back amused. Damn, she's refreshing.

Laying down, I tell her, "Sit that cute, pink pussy on my face, sweetheart."

Raising her leg, she straddles my shoulders, her

little tits lifting up and down with her heavy pants of anticipation.

I haven't even touched her yet, but know she's going to be a firecracker. I can already tell by her eager moans.

Just as she drops her hips and I flick my tongue up to meet her, the door opens and a scream rings out through the room.

The colorful chick scrambles to get up, toppling over and falling to the floor.

I look up to see who joined us, finding a blonde woman staring down at me with her mouth agape.

"What the hell?" she breathes. She looks familiar, but I can't place her in my intoxicated state.

"Nicky, what the hell are you doing?" the woman asks, directing the question to my little rainbow friend.

Nicky?

"Do you know who this is?" She points a finger at me.

Wait, me, what?

"I met him tonight. Why, who is he?" my girl, *Nicky* asks, grabbing at her clothes and pulling them on.

"That's Mr. Masters son," the blonde informs her.

Mr. Masters? I snort a laugh, and my head spins, the vodka doing its job.

"The boss you were boning?" Colorful girl, erm ... Nicky! Squints.

Hold up, what did she say?

"What?" I ask through the haze of alcohol, making my lips form the question tugging at my brain.

"The boss who fired me after his wife caught him fucking me, yes," she snaps, flipping on a light switch, flooding the room in bright white.

Fuck.

It takes a few beats for my eyes to adjust, but seeing her in the light, I do recognize her from Dad's office. Melissa something or other. God, and I just called her fat lips because she has the biggest lips I've ever seen.

She's sexy as hell, older than me, but still young and fuckable.

Shit, I have a one tracked mind, what did she just say?

"Get out. And tell your father I'm filing a lawsuit for wrongful dismissal."

Snorting, I drag my ass to my feet and saunter past her.

"Tell him yourself, sweetheart. I ain't telling that prick shit."

"Hey, he doesn't have to go. It isn't his fault his dad's a dick."

"Nicky!" the blonde growls.

"It's fine. I've lost my appetite anyway." A smirk tugs up my lips as I wave goodbye.

I don't know where the fuck I am, but I start walking, letting the knowledge sink in that my dad's a cheating piece of shit and my poor mother knew.

Shit, not only knew, but caught him in the act.

No wonder she left us. We both failed her.

Waking up on the front lawn just outside the gates of our house, I groan at the headache forming in my skull and the fact that I'm fucking shoeless.

What the hell?

I don't even remember getting back here.

I force myself to my feet, every muscle in my body protesting the movement. I'm a sweaty mess with drool down my chin.

Sensing eyes on me, I take a quick look around, then blow on my hands to remove the debris from them before waving to our neighbor across the street out collecting his newspaper.

"Morning, Mr. Denzel," I rasp at the old fossil.

He looks over at me, a frown marring his wrinkled face.

"You've been there since I woke at four a.m.," he croaks.

Damn. Fucker could have tossed a sheet on me or woke me up. I could have been eaten by wildlife.

The walk up the drive feels like the green mile, my bones mimicking those of an eighty-year-old.

The front door is open when I test the handle, and the chill from the AC blasts over my skin, stinging my flesh. I'm going to need a shower to clean the sticky dew off my skin.

I move through the foyer and come to a halt when I see my dad sitting at the breakfast bar in the kitchen. His head is in his hands as he looks down at what looks like paperwork.

Sensing he's not alone, he looks up through his lashes at me standing in the doorway.

His brows pinch together, and he exhales a ragged breath.

"You look like shit. Where the fuck have you been?" He picks up a glass of what looks like freshly squeezed orange juice and takes a hearty gulp.

My mouth waters at the sight of it. I need some of that.

"Out."

He grits his teeth, his jaw ticking with annoyance.

Placing a hand on the papers in front of him, he slides them across the counter in the direction of where I'm standing.

"Your mother wants a divorce."

He says divorce like it's a curse word, *beneath him.*

"Robbie's death ruined us," he adds, and a ghost hand slides up my spine, making me shiver.

Anger, raw and volatile, burns inside me.

"Or could be the bitch she caught you fucking?" I grunt. His mouth gapes as I turn and take the stairs two at a time.

I need a shower and to get out of here.

SIX

I scoop mash on to my plate, then look over to a bored looking God, who's checking his cell phone, ignoring his father talking to him.

"Once a month, I ask for dinner," Mr. Goddard aka Four scoffs.

"I'm here, aren't I?" God grins over the top of his cell phone.

Rolling his eyes, Four turns his attention to me. There's this air about him that makes my back straighten.

He holds an authority in his posture alone, and his tone commands the room. Despite being a huge-ass motherfucker who weighs in at three-hundred-plus pounds and can barely move, there's something about him that demands respect. I think they call it money.

"Tell me, Rhett, how is your mother?" he asks before

sucking the meat off his chicken bone. Grease slides down one of his chins, and I suppress a shudder.

Fuck. I didn't know he was going to ask me that, and it throws me off.

Gathering my thoughts, I lay my fork down and wipe my mouth with a napkin.

"We don't speak much, sir. But I hope she's well."

Scowl lines crease his forehead, and he leans back in his seat, the creak loud as it protests against his weight.

"I'm sorry to hear that. I bumped into her while I was in New York on business. She seems well. Considering everything she's been through."

Stab to my gut.

"She mentioned college. You've decided to go into law?" He sips straight whiskey from a glass, and smiles over at me.

God and I have been friends since kindergarten, so it's no surprise he and my mother would have spoken about college; it's the invite to his monthly dinner that has my mind working overtime.

It's not a coincidence the police investigation into the fire was squashed a couple days ago. Ruled an "accident." *God works in mysterious ways...*

"What does your father think about you wanting to go into law?" he asks, not waiting for an answer to his former question.

"He uses money for my tuition as a way to keep me in line. He hates that I'm going into law and not finance like him, so he keeps my future dangling on a thread."

God flicks his eyes over to me, then back to his father.

The atmosphere thickens.

"I'm hoping to get into The Elite," I blurt out.

God chokes on his drink and sputters through a coughing fit. His father, though, remains as cool as a cucumber, no surprise in his features.

"Is that a club?" he asks, looking me directly in the eye.

His steel eyes hold mine, until I look away.

"Of sorts." I smile tightly.

"Right. I'm done," God announces, getting to his feet. "You coming?" He rounds the table, stopping next to my chair.

"Sure."

"It was a pleasure seeing you, Rhett. Don't be a stranger around here." Four clears his throat and stands.

"I won't, sir."

He holds out his meaty hand to me, which I stare at for a few seconds in awe before grabbing firmly and giving him a shake.

"I think you'd be an asset to any club."

My chest pounds, and I lock my jaw to prevent myself from getting emotional. It's pathetic, but I respect this man. To have him say that stirs pride inside me.

"Thank you, sir."

SEVEN

Music. Alcohol. Women.

That's how most nights end up for me, and last night was no different.

I need the noise to quiet the voice screaming at me from the back of my subconscious.

The burn of alcohol is becoming an addiction—a necessity to scald away the chill in my veins.

And women to convince me I'm still alive. Breathing and not numb.

Sheets tangle around my limbs like vines, trapping me to the mattress I passed out on last night.

Flashes of the night's activities snap behind my eyelids like movie clips.

Cracking my eyes open, I ignore the sting from the intrusion of light streaming in from the open window and glimpse around the room, recognizing my shit everywhere.

Thank fuck.

That's a good sign. Too many times I've woken up in a stranger's place surrounded by the sin of the night before.

I pat my hands over my body. Naked, all except the condom still attached to my now soft dick.

Gross.

That's sloppy of me.

Usually, I'd ditch that shit and watch the water swirl with it until I knew for sure it was gone. I don't want any little Rhett's out there in the world. One is more than enough.

But I know there are no fluids in it anyway.

Ever since losing Robbie, my body and mind rage war, and my mind always wins. I never allow myself to finish.

The chicks don't notice. Hell, they don't care. As long as they get to say they were fucked by Rhett Masters, that's enough for them.

Sounds stupid, shallow, but it's true. And something I was proud of before…

My entire high school years were built on my reputation of panty peeler, pussy realtor, heart stealer.

People wanted to either be me, or get with me, it was as simple as that.

Money mixed with athletic ability and good looks equals power.

What can I say, humans are basic creatures, and I'd grown a reputation I wasn't ready to give up yet.

It's all I have left.

LUST

A pounding on the bedroom door causes a groan to pass my lips and kicks off a marching band in my skull.

Cotton balls fill my mouth as an acid stream crawls up my throat, threatening to expel last night's liquor intake.

"Fuck off," I bark out, wincing when the door is flung open and crashes against the foundations, rattling the mirror fixed to the far wall.

"Or come in," I grit out under my breath.

I hate living here, especially when he's playing *dad*, like he actually gives a fuck about me or what I do.

Morning to you too, Dad.

He glares at me, disdain in his dark brown eyes. If I could fully open my own, I'd reflect that look back at him.

I remind him of my mother, and he won't admit it, but he hates me because of it. He still loves her, and I'm a constant reminder of what he's lost. Not just her, but his favorite son too. Now, all he has is me, and I can't stand him.

"Are you listening to me?" His voice booms, wrenching me from the ghosts that own my mind.

No.

His cell shrills from his pocket, giving me a reprieve from his disturbance.

Exhaling an exhausted breath, he flees from the doorway to talk in mumbled whispers to whoever the fuck is calling this early.

No doubt one of his hoes. He's made no effort to cover up his whoring ways now that he knows I know he cheated. Dick.

Caught balls deep in his secretary, yet tried to blame

his divorce on Robbie's death. He makes me sick.

His fucking secretary?

Ten years younger and dumb as shit, thinking if she let him dip his old dick in her cunt, it would propel her career.

Cliché as fuck.

People say love is powerful, and that's true, but more often than not, it's corrupted by lust.

Lust is a force all its own. It consumes the mind and body, and causes even the most loyal to indulge in its sinful ways. He risked it all for a quick fuck over his desk.

He didn't think of the chaos that *fuck* would cause.

Lust is a violent desire, destructive and uncontrollable. If you let the sensation take root, you become captive to its power, until you're waking up in the wreckage of its path.

And even though it's part of the reason Mom left, I would still take lust over love every fucking time.

Fuck love.

It's more damaging to the soul than anything else in the world.

Losing someone you love is like living through your own death.

The pain so brutal, the sorrow rips the soul to shreds while still pumping gas to the heart.

No big brother should have to see his kid brother die.

No parent should have to outlive their child—bury their child.

Grief is a fickle whore. It hits me in waves, reminding me whenever I try to forget. The remorse chasing me, and I can't outrun it, no matter how reckless I become.

"I won't be late, I promise."

I am the fucking cliché

"If I hadn't seen the three girls sneaking out of here, I'd start to worry about you two." My old man shakes his head, sneering down at something on my floor as he returns to my doorframe, disdain in his tone.

Lifting to my elbows, I follow his glare and snort.

God, my best friend and partner in crime is sprawled out on the floor, buck ass naked, with a pair of panties over his head covering his eyes.

"Don't be a homophobe, Dad. How do you know we don't just let the women watch?" I tease, just to see the disgust transform his features.

Redneck piece of shit.

I wanted to be nothing like him growing up. Robbie was his little double. Used to sit in his office for hours learning the ropes of trading.

Our old man liked to play the hotshot, and he was rich, but it was our mother's money and power that shrunk his junk. He blew the only thing he ever did right, *marrying her,* by letting his ego and dick control things.

My mother was one of the most popular residents and business owners in this town, inherited properties from her own father, and now can't stand to be here. She fled, leaving me at the mercy of my merciless father.

"Get dressed and get out. School starts today. I had to pull too many strings to even get you in there, so all this shit has to stop. I can only do so much before I just wipe my hands with you, boy."

He says "boy" with a growl, and I offer him the middle finger, then flop back on my pillow. The soft cushion cocoons my hangover.

I intend to earn my mother's respect back, make her proud, and make my father regret ever telling me I'd amount to nothing and it should have been me who died that night.

That's something we can agree on, but it's not how it is.

Studying law will be my new promise to his memory. I'll make sure fuckers don't get off so lightly when they tear apart lives.

"Rhett," Dad barks again, alerting me to the fact that he didn't take my middle finger salute as a hint to fuck off.

"Move your ass, and for God's sake, put some clothes on."

The door slams closed, and God lifts his head from the floor.

"Did he say my name?"

Grinning, I throw my pillow at God's head.

"Dick." He grumbles.

Time to get up. Untangling myself I shift out the bed to my feet before trailing my ass into the shower.

I didn't need him riding my ass. I have no intention of fucking up on my first day.

There's shit I need to prove.

Catching my image in the mirror, I groan. My dark irises are accompanied by red specks discoloring the whites of my eyes.

My full lips are dried out, and my mop of brown waves is sticking up in every fucking direction imaginable.

Rubbing a hand over my torso, I notice I've dropped some weight lately, making my six-pack look more shredded. I need to eat more.

"You finished checking yourself out?" God snorts,

sauntering into the bathroom and taking a piss.

"I look like shit," I grunt, flicking the shower on and allowing the steam to fill the space.

"I've been telling you that for years. The chicks disagree, though. What can you do?" he mocks, shaking his junk and leaving me to it.

I step under the shower spray, and the water punishes down on me a degree below scolding. I allow the heat to cleanse me of my sins from the night before while trying to conjure up the memory of who I was with, but the women all blur into one.

God was right about the chicks seeing gold where I saw copper. I don't know why they fuck with me, but they can't get enough. It doesn't matter whether I even remember their names the next day.

I've always been a party boy.

Captain of the football team, wealthy, and according to my English teacher, "stupidly good looking."

That's what she panted as she pawed at me while I fucked her on her desk the last day of summer school.

She'd been begging for it since she saw me changing in the corridor one time.

Her subtle looks and excuses keeping me behind after class made it obvious she wanted a taste, so I gave it to her, and she gave me the grade I needed.

Everyone wanted a taste, and I'd always been keen to give it to them—until recently. I'd lost my urges since my brother's death. Sexual gratification reminded me too much of why I was late that night, and as much as I play the part of being the lust-filled pussy-chaser, there's a crater size hole in my chest threatening to consume me at any given moment.

God got me through each day still breathing. He has his own issues, and together, we're a lethal fucking mix of chaos and sin.

"You wearing that?" God smirks when I leave the bathroom fully dressed in suit pants, a shirt, and tie, my dark hair contained with hair wax, giving me a professional look instead of the just-dried-straight-from-the-shower look I usually rock.

"Getting into The Elite is my only way out from under my dad's money and fucking guardianship. I need them to help me get the man who killed my brother. I need to look the part," I remind him.

"Dude, looking like some preppy geek won't get you into The Elite. You've already laid the groundwork, you need me to talk to my dad?"

"No, it's cool"

It was my dad that was the problem.

My brush with the law after burning down the post office nearly tarnished our family name in the eyes of my dad, now he was being a dick.

What he didn't know was that my brush with the law was all part of me laying the ground work to be chosen for the Elite.

Dad said it was a close call and one he wasn't taking lightly.

"It's a miracle they're ruling it an accident."

But I knew better. It was no miracle; The Elite fixed the problem.

The Elite could take care of my tuition and give me the means to set myself up in my own place, sever the parental rights, and free me. And get me the information I need on the prick who killed Robbie and help me take him down. He fucking deserves more punishment than a tiny fine.

EIGHT

Gulping down the rest of my breakfast in the form of a giant energy drink, I tap my fingers on the steering wheel, trying to build up the balls to get out of the car.

It's a strange sensation being out of my comfort zone, especially in a school type environment.

God was right about the outfit. Not one person here was dressed in anything other than casual clothes. I'm glad he made me bring a change of outfit.

"Wanna meet up for lunch?" I turn my attention to God, who napped the entire way here and is now scrolling through his cell phone, yawning. He's all or nothing—either speed-balling on whatever upper he can get his hands on or dragging when he crashes.

"Nah, man. I've got some shit to do. We can catch up tonight."

Frowning, I grab his cell and turn the thing off.

"Dude, what the fuck?" he grinds out, holding his hand out to me.

"You not going to class?"

He snorts and snatches his phone back.

"No one goes to class freshman week."

Opening the car door, he slides out and salutes me.

I follow suit, calling out, "Why the fuck did you ride here then?"

Grinning, he turns to walks backwards, stating. "To support you…and I didn't want to be left with your old man. He looks at me weird. I think he's got a crush."

I give him the finger, and he chuckles, jogging out the parking lot.

The slacks I'm wearing are crushing my ball sac, and the tie feels like a noose around my neck. Why the fuck did I think I could pull this shit off.

Popping the trunk, I grab my bag, then open it up pulling out my clothes.

God knows me better than I know myself half the time, I lasted a whole car ride before needing to change.

I whip my tie off, then unbutton my shirt, giving a quick look around the parking lot. There are a few bodies lurking around, but fuck it.

Tugging my pants down, I ignore a guy standing a few feet away getting out of his car. His eyes expand and give me the once over before he holds his cell phone up and snaps a photo, bold as fuck.

Like there aren't a million pictures of me half naked on the internet.

"Supplies for your spank bank?" I wink, and he blushes before hurrying away, clearly unaware of being caught red-handed. Pervert.

After slipping a pair of black jeans up my legs, I tear off my shirt, replace it with a black tee, and throw on the trusty Tom Ford leather jacket God brought me back from a fashion show his mother was involved in last year.

I close the trunk and hitch my bag up on my shoulder.

Leaning down to see myself in the car window, I run my hands through my hair to mess it up.

This is me, I can't pull off the preppy, put together look.

The rhythm in my chest pounds, and I take in a deep breath. I'm taking back control, yet feel like a boy starting kindergarten for the first time.

The grounds of the college expand beyond what my eyes can take in. It's like a continuous garden covered by an abundance of grass and shrubbery.

Benches sit beneath large billowing trees standing tall and proud against the stone backdrop of the actual building.

I feel out of my depth, and that's unsettling. I've always been in control, held the cards, made the rules, yet, for some fucking reason, I'm anxious as shit.

My whole high school career was to get me to this place, and now I'm here, I know I can't ride the wave of my football fame. That ship sailed without me on board. Getting through college is going to take real work, study, focus, and less fucking around.

Taking a breath, I move farther onto the grounds, taking it all in.

White stone bricks stacked tall into the sky with round pillars like castle turrets make the place look almost mythical, and reaches dizzying heights.

Large decorative windows with arched entryways give a royal vibe. The appearance alone has me gulping. We're not in high school anymore, that's for sure.

Dodging a few kids rushing around like they're late, my eyes fall on a few students handing out flyers to any and everyone including me.

"Yo, bro, download the app," some dude says, pushing a business type card into my hand.

It's weird being on a campus where no one really knows me and treats me like everyone else.

Girls' stares still linger on me, but unlike high school, there isn't a crowd forming around my car to greet me purely based on my mere fucking arrival.

People acknowledge me with a head tilt, but that's it.

I wasn't king of the school anymore.

Nope. No one gives a fuck.

I'm just another rich kid who paid his way in, and that thought unsettled me.

My plans of coming here and being a sure bet for The Elite begin to fade from my view. The mere size of campus alone is daunting.

Whispering doubt siphons into my conscience from my own fear of failure. My mother's words fire into my brain like a machine gun.

"You owe it to him."

The air around me thickens, and the darkness begins creeping into my marrow, taunting me with the ghosts that haunt me.

I would do whatever it takes to become an Elite, but the actual possibility of not getting in has only just dawned on me. The things that matter most to me are the things I have no control over now.

A cold-sweat breaks over my skin, and my chest begins to pound, roaring in my own ears.

There are people rushing past me, their lives put together, their paths laid out and set, and here I am, a fucking mess.

The grounds appear to expand in size before me showing me just how little I matter.

My father's words echo in my thoughts.

"I give him six months before he fucks up and gets kicked out. He's a jock, Caroline, not college potential."

Unlike every other father in history, mine hated that I played football. He didn't want me wasting my brains by getting them knocked out of me on a field. It embarrassed him that I was into sports and not the family businesses.

"Football is for people who have no other choices." He used to scoff at me as he spent my mother's money and worked for a firm her father created and passed down to her.

Just as my lungs begin squeezing the life from them, a soft thud hits my back, and a female topples to the concrete beside me.

Paper rains down around her like confetti, and an "oomph" sounds from her lungs as a book lands on top of her chest with a thump.

Pride and Prejudice.

Jane Eyre.

"Christ," she squeaks out, looking up at me with wide, clear eyes, a perfectly formed O on her full, thick lips.

"I'm so sorry," she quickly says, rubbing her palms together before removing the book and picking up the paper, shoving it inside the pages.

Dropping to my haunches, I help collect her papers, my eyes roaming briefly over one.

It's a flyer for a book club. Meetings on a Saturday. Who the fuck goes to book club on a Saturday?

"I honestly should look where I'm going. I'm clumsy, and was so engrossed in my book—then *bang, whoosh*. And now I'm sitting on the ground mumbling to the most prettiest guy I've ever seen."

She laughs awkwardly, blushing a wild red and then covering her mouth to try to shove the words back inside.

I raise a brow, and her eyes expand behind red-framed glasses. "Did I say that out loud?"

A chuckle rumbles from my chest, and it's then I realize she knocked my panic attack right out of me.

Blonde messy curls cascade down her shoulders, stopping at her tits hidden inside a blouse covered by a pink fluffy sweater. Creamy legs spill from underneath a black skirt that's ridden up her thighs. Flat ballerina pumps finish her outfit. It's cute, bookish, but with a hidden sultry vibe that comes from her peaches and cream skin, just enough on show to entice, but not enough to make her look slutty.

I move back up her body and catch her eyes watching me.

Large, oval blue eyes take up her heart-shaped face. They're almost violet and dancing with curiosity. Her petite nose wrinkles, tugging up her full top lip.

"Hey," she finally says, offering me her hand.

"Rhett Masters." I take her small hand in mine and shake it.

A crease forms on her forehead. "From Garden Grove High School?" She poses it as a question, but recognition sparks in her blue eyes.

"I guess I'm not as unknown here as I thought." I wink down at her, and she doesn't do what every other female in my life has done.

She doesn't melt.

Well, fuck me.

NINE

Getting to her feet, she dusts down her skirt, then hugs the book to her chest like a Rhett-proof vest.

"You have me at a disadvantage, sweetness." I lay on the charm, swiping my tongue out to wet my lips. She watches the movement, and the rosy tint to her flesh spreads down her neck.

If I were to open her blouse, I bet it would be all the way down to her tits, making her nipples tingle.

"You played our football team last summer. It was a charity sports thing, otherwise I would have never attended."

She wrinkles her nose again, but this time, in disgust, like she's smelled something that offended her nostrils.

There's something that changed her attitude from apologetic, almost flirty, to grievance. Maybe it's Football, or rather a football player—me. Did we beat her team? We beat every team.

"And?" I coax. I played a lot of games and need her to elaborate on this one.

Tucking a strand of hair behind her ear, she pushes her glasses up her nose and looks at her toes.

"You hooked up with my best friend, then never called her." She frowns gathering her pieces of paper from my hand and stuffing them with the rest.

I rub a hand through my hair, a soft shrug lifting my shoulder. It makes her flinch. It's slight, but she's uncomfortable, or even pissed, at my response.

"Not going to lie, sweetheart. I don't do the whole calling thing, and I would have made that clear to your friend before I fucked her."

A gasp whooshes from her, and she shakes her head, her petite, little nose wrinkling once more. It's cute as fuck.

She's like some sexy, innocent librarian type. It's not what I'd usually go for, but there is no denying her beauty.

"I said hooked up, not…what you said."

"Fucked," I offer, just to see the flush of her skin.

She doesn't let me down. Perfect.

I bet that's the same color she turns after she comes. My thoughts turn to picturing her naked, and I wonder if the blonde curls are a theme for every part of her.

"She didn't do that with you," she snaps, demanding my focus.

I hold my hands up in surrender. Damn, this girl needs to chill out. Since when did hook-up not mean fucking? And since when was saying fuck offensive?

"Well, great to meet you…?"

"Chastity," she almost whispers.

Of course that's her name. A grin lifts my lips as I walk backwards a few steps so I can commit all those curves to my memory. It's been a while since lustful thoughts have taken root in my mind, and it almost makes me feel like the old me.

By the time I get inside, the halls are quiet, with only a few people milling around. I check my watch, and then the map I was given by some high-on-life dude at the entrance.

My hands are loaded with a hundred other flyers shoved at me by students recruiting for frat houses, roommates, and party invitations. Unlike high school, no one appears to be excluded from the parties. Every person who walked by had the papers pushed into their hands.

I navigate the corridor and come to the counselor's office. Best to get this over with.

Rapping my knuckles on the door, I ignore the pounding of my heart in my chest. I didn't want to do this—didn't want to talk about things. *About him.*

"Come in," a feminine voice calls out, and as I push open the door the idea of being able to seduce a female so I don't have to share crosses my mind.

A slim, petite woman stands to greet me, and I'm taken back by how youthful she appears. In truth, I was expecting some old dude, but this woman has to be in her thirties at most—and she's hot.

Black hair the color of spilled ink is sleeked back into a high ponytail, cat like eyes look over me with intrigue, and thin, red-painted lips offer a hint of a smile as she introduces herself.

"I'm Mrs. Griffin, but I allow students to call me Lillian."

Griffin...wasn't the dean's name Griffin?

"Yes," she answers my unasked question.

"I'm the dean's wife, but I assure you that doesn't affect my job. Anything you say to me doesn't get spoken of outside this room, unless I believe you're a danger to yourself or others."

She's sitting behind her desk, her hands placed in her lap.

"Okay," is all I say. This feels awkward as hell.

She gestures to the chair on the opposite side of her desk. "Please, take a seat."

Dropping my bag to the floor, I sit my ass in the chair and take in the scenery.

The room is filled with natural light from the tall ass window.

A filing cabinet dominates the back wall, but other than that, it's minimal décor and spacious. Her desk is positioned in the center of the room, and her chair is stupidly large. She looks like a child perched on a throne.

"So, Mr. Masters, Rhett, do you prefer to be called by your forename or is there another name you go by?"

Most chicks call me Romeo.

"Rhett's fine." I nod.

"Okay. Is there anything you'd like to talk about today, Rhett?"

"No, I'm good," I tell her, and an uncomfortable silence ensues.

She definitely got this job because of her husband. She seems out of her depth.

Shifting in her chair, she reads over a piece of paper on her desk, then looks up at me.

"How are you feeling about your classes? You attended summer school to get your grades up? Do you want to tell me why they slipped in the first place?"

No. Why the fuck do they ask questions they already know the answers to?

"I'm sure if that information is on that piece of paper, then so are the reasons why."

She narrows her eyes briefly, then smiles and nods her head.

"Yes, it does, but I want to hear the answer from you."

"Why?"

"So I can understand you better."

Sharp pains stab at my heart as flashes of that night race to the forefront of my mind.

"I got my brother killed and it fucked me up," I state, irritated.

She looks like she's trying to frown, but her forehead doesn't move.

Folding her arms on the desk, she asks, "You feel like you're to blame?"

"It was my fault." I shrug. Emotions wash through me, leaving an angry buzz behind.

"Do we have to talk about this shit? It's the first day, and I don't want to miss my first class."

Looking at her watch, she smiles over at me.

"I'm sorry. You're right. We can discuss this another time. I wanted you to come in and see me because I know how daunting it can be when your life choices change, especially in such a dramatic way."

She points to something on the sheet of paper. "You were a ball player, but got an injury and decided to go into law?"

"I want to help people get justice when the system robs them of it."

"So, it's personal." She smiles.

"You could say that."

"Well, that's another discussion for another day. I've recruited a mentor of sorts to help you settle in and help show you around your first week here. If for any reason you want to talk, my door is always open. You're on my calendar for bi-weekly appointments that are mandatory, I'm afraid. If I don't see you before our next appointment, I hope you have a good start to the school year."

With that, a soft knock sounds at the door and she gets to her feet.

"Right on time."

Walking around her desk, she goes to the door, and I follow suit.

Blonde curls enter the room, and I bite the inside of my cheek to stop from grinning.

Chastity's eyes enlarge before narrowing on me.

"This is Chastity. Chastity, Rhett Masters," she introduces.

I hold my hand out, but she doesn't take it. "We've met," she informs Lillian.

"Oh…well, that's a great start. I have an appointment, so enjoy your day." Lillian's eyes cut to a tall, dark haired guy who looks a little out of place in his surroundings. His appearance and style harder, more rogue than rich like the rest of the students on campus. His eyes clash with mine briefly before, without a word or instruction, he gets up and disappears into Lillian's office.

Following Chastity into the corridor, I hold my hands up once more in surrender.

"I've clearly made the wrong impression, and I think it's unfair of you to judge me on something I did in the past with someone I don't even remember."

Her face screws into a hateful scowl, and she shocks me into silence when she raises her hand and flicks the tip of my nose. "You're a jerk."

I'm still standing there seconds later watching her ass sashay up the corridor without me.

Some mentor she is.

TEN

God's casual remark about no one attending class freshman week doesn't appear to be the case.

My first class is packed. The door slams behind me as I enter, bringing all eyes to me. The professor stops talking and watches me as I make a spectacle of myself, trying to dodge legs and bags to get one of the only available seats right in the center of the room.

Perfect.

When I finally do plant my ass in the seat, the professor folds his arms and paces the front of the room.

"First thing I want you to know, you're not in high school anymore. No tardy slips or toilet passes. I expect you to be independent, responsible, and punctual."

His eyes seek me out, and he glares right at me when he says, "Nothing makes a bad impression like strolling in late."

He then looks around at the other students and smiles. "It also makes finding a seat a nightmare."

Laughs ring out, mocking me, and I offer him a tight smile as I get out my laptop and nod.

Understood. First lesson learned. Check.

A light flicks on a white board, then a list appears with titles of books we're going to need to read for this semester.

He must like the sound of his own voice because he spends the next hour talking about how he ended up a professor here. By the time we're leaving the classroom, I've already made a pact with myself to arrive early to every class I have from here on out.

The day passes without any run-ins with the lovely Chastity or any whispers about The Elite. Not that I expected them to be advertising themselves.

Checking my cell and ignoring all the texts apart from God's, I dial his number. He answers on the third ring, and by the sound of the bad line, I know he's driving.

"Where've you been?"

"The gym. I'm leaving, though. Meet me at Dad's."

He ends the call, giving me no fucking choice.

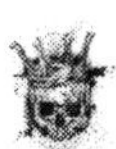

When I pull up to God's, the entrance gate is open, which usually means one thing: God's parents are out of town and he's planning to throw a party. He lives in town, but likes to throw parties at his parents' house since it's so fucking huge. Plus, when it's all over, he makes the staff clean up.

The long, winding driveway bordered by large, towering oak trees takes at least ten seconds to drive up before the house even comes into view. My parents are wealthy, but God's are stupid rich—own their own plane rich—and God is their only child. Raised by a money hungry power couple, and because of that, God loved everything in excess.

He has a garage full of cars most people couldn't even dream of owning in their lifetime, and he's only eighteen and has yet to even make his mark in the business world.

Their house is a plantation home built in the 1700s, with balconies for each of the sixteen bedrooms, multiple garages, pool houses, and acres of land.

Pulling my car up next to his Ferrari, I jump out and bound up the stairs to his front door, which is open. I call out his name, and my voice echoes, bouncing off the oak wood floors and down the corridor. A few beats later, a shuffling of feet come toward me in the shape of Wendy, the Goddard's wonderful, loyal, housekeeper.

Many times, this woman has kept food in my belly and clean clothes on my back when I'd push my luck at home and needed to crash here throughout the years.

"Rhett, my darling boy, it's so good to see you. You're looking too skinny, let me feed you," she says in a comforting tone that reminds me of my late grandmother.

"How are you, Wendy? I haven't seen you at any parties lately," I tease, and she rewards me with a tap to my arms and an amused smile.

Guiding me through the house and into the kitchen, she gestures for me to take a seat at the breakfast bar.

"Where's God?" I ask, accepting the glass of fresh lemonade.

"He's taking a shower. He came back all covered in this dirt that will never come out of his clothes." She rolls her eyes, waving a frustrated hand between unloading the fridge with the makings of a sandwich.

I don't even want to know why he was covered in dirt. God is the craziest son of a bitch I know, and sometimes it's best not knowing. If I don't know, no one can ask me about it. That was a best friend pact we made way back when.

And it worked for us. We tell each other shit that's important, but other than that, need to know is best.

"Here, eat." Wendy pushes a sandwich in my direction.

I offer her a grateful smile and take my sandwich up to Gods' room with me.

The shower hums from his en suite, steam creeping around the open door.

I take a bite of the sandwich, and my stomach growls. This is the first time I've eaten since a candy bar at lunch.

Dumping my bag on his computer desk, I slump down on his bed, ignoring the pull of the mattress beckoning me to take a nap.

A pile of rumpled up clothes dumped in his trashcan grabs my attention, and I put down the plate with my half-eaten sandwich and pick up the sweater God left wearing this morning.

Stains paint the white material, but it's not dirt, it's blood.

My cell buzzes with a notification from one of the party apps I added today, and I snort.

The address is God's house. I fucking knew he was going to throw a party. How the fuck did he get this out there? He wasn't even on campus today.

Hearing the shower turn off and his feet pad across the floor, I hold up his sweater.

Pausing briefly when he enters the room and sees me, he places his hands on his hips, waiting for the questions he knows is coming.

"Wendy said you had dirt stains on your clothes. This isn't dirt."

Raising a brow, he walks over to me, wearing only a small towel wrapped around his waist, flashing his junk at me.

"Wendy's blind as a bat."

"Dude, I wish I was." I fake offense. Turning my head, I throw the sweater at him to cover his junk. I'd seen God's junk as much as my own over the years, but I want to lighten the mood.

"So, you want to tell me what this is about?"

"Nothing to tell. Not my blood." He smirks, swiping my unfinished sandwich and scarfing it.

"You know I'd back you no matter what shit you get into right? You're my brother before anything else," I say, just putting it out there.

Dropping the towel, he slips a pair of jeans up his legs and runs a hand through his wet hair.

"Some prick didn't like losing to me. He got mouthy, so I closed it for him."

That sounds about right. God took shit from no one. People usually knew better than to even attempt it.

"How the fuck did you manage to get a party sorted without even coming to class today?" I ask, throwing myself back on his bed. I want to crash so bad. I've burned myself out.

"We want to make ourselves known, get people talking, establish ourselves amongst our peers."

He's right, like always. If I want my name spread amongst The Elite, I need to mingle with potential members. A party is perfect.

My eyes close briefly, but Robbie meets me there, causing a cold shiver to race up my spine.

"You want to take a nap?" God questions, but I've already opened my eyes and gotten to my feet.

"Nah. I'll grab a shower, though."

ELEVEN

How the fuck God pulls off parties to this extreme on a whim is beyond me.

A live band plays from the lounge area, food and drinks are served by waitstaff, and the place is almost at capacity.

Wading through the bodies of our peers, I greet people with a head nod and make my way to the pool out back, knowing there'll be kegs out there.

I'm spent and in need of sleep, but before I can give in to the exhaustion, I have to place a wall up in my mind, and each drink I consume adds a brick to that wall, blocking out the thoughts. *Nightmares.*

A beer gets handed to me as I step outside by a waitress carrying a tray of red cups. It's the stupidest shit I've ever seen, but I accept the drink and reach for another.

Music filters through the open doors with well-placed speakers, extending the party to the open grounds. God's house could host a music festival if he wanted. I'm surprised this hasn't happened already.

"I can't escape you." A huffed voice penetrates my ear from behind me.

Turning toward the sound, a grin tugs up my lips. There must be a hundred people out here, yet she stands out amongst them all.

"Or you're stalking me. Don't you have books to read?" I tease, chugging the contents of the first cup, then the second, trying my best not to look over Chastity's figure that's been squeezed into a tight, black, sparkly dress.

I fail.

Her hair is pulled up off her face, and she's not wearing her glasses. The contacts make her eyes appear brighter, even under the dim light of the moon. I'm not sure which look I like best on her. I think she could wear a sack and make it appealing.

My eyes chase the creamy hollow of her elegant neck and rest on the plump mounds of her cleavage on display. A small freckle sits in the valley of her cleavage, and my mind traces the path with my tongue, wanting to strip away the fabric from her skin and see if she has more freckles elsewhere.

I know I'm failing at feigning disinterest in her body, but fuck, she's all kinds of beautiful, and her attitude just makes me want to break her down and make her beg for my touch.

I raise my eyes to hers. There's a silence cloaking us, despite the music and chatter around us. It's like we've been sucked into a vacuum and no one else exists.

The moment doesn't last when a redhead saddles up next to her, almost startling her from the hypnotic hold I held her in. The newcomer offers Chastity a glass of what I assume is wine by the color, but she declines with a subtle head shake. The girl shrugs a shoulder and studies me with an intrigue I'm used to receiving from the opposite sex—hell, even the same sex.

"You know my best friend, Maggie," Chastity snaps, narrowing those blues on me. I bite my lip and count to ten in my head to stop myself from throwing her over my shoulder and fucking all that defiance out of her. Looking to her friend, I try to conjure up recognition, but nothing comes to me. She's shorter than Chastity and carries more weight around her ass and hips, which she crammed into too-small jeans.

"No, we haven't had the pleasure," the girl answers for me with a seductive purr, pushing herself forward and offering me her hand.

"Rhett." I take her hand and give it a kiss, just to enjoy the tsking I'm gifted from Chastity.

"This is Rhett Masters, Maggie. Remember?" Chastity grinds out my name like it's an offensive slur.

A hand snakes around my shoulder, and God crowds into my space, leaning in to whisper in my ear. "I need to take off for a bit. You good holding shit down here?"

"That's Rhett Masters," the redhead growls, pointing her pink painted nail at God.

God doesn't even pay her any attention and just waits for me to nod my head in response to the question he asked. As soon as he has the confirmation he needs, he slips into the sea of people and out of sight.

"Huh. He didn't even acknowledge me," Maggie exhales.

"That's not Rhett, Maggie," Chastity informs her, annoyance in her tone.

There's visible embarrassment coloring Chasity's cheeks. Part of me wants to let her off the hook for hating on me today when in fact it was God her best friend hooked up with. But she brings out the pettiness in me, so instead, I fold my arms and shake my head at her. "Bet you feel pretty stupid right about now?"

The redhead looks between the two of us, then backs away. "I'm going to get us some drinks." She slinks over to a bar set up on the other side of the pool area, leaving her friend and me in a stare off.

"You want to start your apology now, or do you need time to study how to?"

She turns to look at anything but me, folding her arms and prodding her inner cheek with her tongue.

"So, she made a mistake. It could have easily been you. You look alike," she defends eventually.

Tutting my tongue, I purse my lips. "That's a really shit apology and argument. You think that would hold up in court? He could have been the one to murder those people because he looks like the man who actually did it, so charge him anyway."

Dropping her arms, she screws up her pretty features. "That got dark."

"You're dancing around the point."

"That point is moot. You proved yourself to be a pig after the initial hook-up fiasco."

Feigning hurt, I hold a hand over my heart. "Your words have the power to hurt, Chastity. Not me, because I think you're a stuck-up bitch—but they could hurt someone, someday."

A pain shoots up my shin, and it takes me a few seconds to realize she kicked me.

"Did you just kick me in the shin like a five-year-old?" I snort.

She balls her tiny hands into fists at her side. "Yep. Don't call me a bitch. If I had a drink right now, you'd be wearing it."

I open my mouth to accuse her of being a brat when arms encase my waist from behind and a warm, small body pushes against my back. Then a voice I recognize croons, "Romeo, Romeo where are thee." Sunny Bishop slides around my torso and pins herself to my side.

"It's where art thou," Chastity scoffs, rolling her eyes.

"Oh, I'm sorry, Shakespeare." Sunny laughs, loud and high-pitched "Who's the textbook?" Sunny looks up at me, trying her best to offer me a seductive smile.

I haven't seen her since school ended, and she's all up on me like she's my girl or some shit.

Turning on her heel to leave, Chastity smirks and mimes, "Bye, Romeo," waggling her fingers.

Separating Sunny from my body, I push her away and reach for Chastity's arm before she can flee completely. Her breath hitches as I swing her back to face me, our bodies almost touching. I can taste her scent infecting my senses and know it will refuse to leave long after she's gone.

"You owe me something," I remind her. Her eyes explore every inch of my face, then suddenly, she's jolted from the side and falls. Wide eyes expand, and thick lips form a huge O as she tries to catch herself, but fails, pulling my arms down with her. It all happens too quick for me to react, to tighten my hold to save us both. In the next instant, cold water sloshes around us as we submerge, the liquid depths consuming us both and robbing me of breath.

I break the surface of the pool, gasping for air. My stupid hair sticks to my forehead and blinds me. Swiping a hand over my face to clear it, I search for her to surface. When she does, she lets out a shaky screech. "You pushed me."

Sunny points down at us and cackles like a fucking witch. "Ooops, sorry," she mocks, smirking.

"Pool party," some drunk dickhead shouts, and bodies begin hitting the water.

I'm not drunk enough for this shit. "You want to come inside and get out of that?" I offer Chastity, but the heat I felt from her briefly is fucking ice cold now, and the hate grimace is back on her pretty face.

"Eat a bag of dicks," she snaps, then attempts to blow hair from her face with no avail.

"Why a whole bag? That's just wrong," I counter.

"You're just wrong. Stay away from me." She shudders, goosebumps sprinkling over her flesh.

"Whatever, ice princess."

Pulling myself from the pool, I strip down to my boxers to the catcalls of partygoers and leave my wet clothes where I stand.

Fuck it. Time to numb the senses.

My buzz is strong from a round of shots placed on the counter inside. I'm slightly unsteady on my feet and find myself moving to the beat of some chick playing through the speakers or a mic or whatever. I stuff another piece of meat in my face from one of the many plates lurking around. The crowd has thinned a little, but everyone is in high spirits drinking, dancing, and making out.

The pool is full of idiots. Far back in my mind I know I should tell them to get out, but fuck it.

"Why are you naked?" God asks, coming through the front door stone-cold sober. Where the fuck has he been all night? I look down at myself. I'm still wearing my boxers, which are now dry. "Sunny pushed me in the pool," I hiccup.

"Okay," is all he says, disappearing through to the rec room.

I want to go after him and ask where he's been, but I need to piss.

Making it up the stairs, clicking of stilettos follow. Without looking, I know it's Sunny. She's had her eyes on me all night like a creeper waiting in the shadows for their prey to be drunk enough to seduce.

I bypass the main guest bathroom and make my way to God's room, opening the door and leaving it ajar for her to follow.

"I thought you were going to leave me hanging all night." She closes the door behind her and traces my steps over to the bed.

Raking my gaze over her, they drop to the bottle of Jim Beam, she's carrying, waggling it in her hand at me like it's a prize I've won.

Unscrewing the cap, she saunters the last few steps,

trying to tempt me into more than the drink. She's hot, always has been, but gets clingy, so I've never re-visited our one time together despite her best efforts.

"You want?" She licks her lips before taking a sip of the bottle. She then leans forward and dribbles the amber fire into my mouth.

That's hot.

Pushing against my shoulders, she guides me to lay back on the bed, parts my knees, and slides between them.

I take the bottle from her and chug until every part of my throat and stomach fills with lava.

My thoughts are swimming in the high, making no sense of anything, and that's good—that's what I need.

Nimble fingers grasp and tug at my boxers, freeing my cock. A warm palm strokes firm and tight along my shaft. There's a voice faint in the back of mind warning me this is a bad idea, but I try to wash it away with the hum of alcohol in my bloodstream.

My dick struggles to gain its usual hard appetite. My fucking brain won't switch off despite Sunny's administrations.

"You want my mouth, Romeo?" Her voice drips with lust, but I just can't fucking focus on this or her. If I were sober, I wouldn't go near her. She caught feelings for me in high school and using her will just make her think there's something here that isn't.

I don't need to use chicks and their infatuations for sexual favors. I can get them from party girls who, like me, just want an escape and a good time.

Willing my groggy brain to focus, I sit up and guide her by the biceps to stand.

"Something wrong, baby?" She presses the pads of her

fingers to her lips, and as much as I want to sort through the right words to say, I'm just too far fucking gone. The haze of drunkenness has me swimming in a black sea without searchlights.

"Romeo?" She chokes up now, and I get to my feet, swaying, and pull my shorts over my ass.

"Can you get out? I need to piss and sleep."

Fuck, I need to sleep.

"What about…?"

"Summer, just go."

Slap.

Motherfucker. Tiny pinpricks expand over my face from her palm hitting my cheek.

Before I even realize they're closed, I'm opening my eyes and narrowing them on her.

"Ow."

"You called me Summer. My name is Sunny. You've known me for six years!"

I walk past her and hold onto the door to steady myself. "It's been fun."

She's pissed. Her arms are now folded under her tits and there's a grimace on her face.

"You're a pig, you know that?" she growls, storming past me.

"Apparently so," I snort, slamming the door behind her ass.

I drag my feet to the bathroom. As soon as I hit the threshold, my heart leaps into my mouth. A figure greets me inside.

"Shit," I breathe, grabbing my chest to make sure my heart didn't just explode.

"I'm not stalking you." Chastity frowns. She's on the

toilet, lid down and a towel wrapped around her body. Her black dress is hanging over the shower door.

"If I'd known you were waiting for me, I'd have come sooner." I smirk, but don't feel it. There's a stirring in my gut.

"Maggie didn't want to leave, so I snuck up here to wait for my dress to dry and for her to be ready. She drove us," she defends.

My stomach contracts, and a groan leaves my lips.

"Are you going to be sick?" she gasps, jumping to her feet. Her hair is still damp, hanging in ringlets around her face.

All makeup has been removed by the water, or maybe some of God's products. She's bare, and her voice is oddly soothing.

"No." I shake my head. "I need to lay down. Will you talk to me for a couple minutes?"

"What? Why?" she scoffs.

My brow furrows, and the liquor in my veins offers her truth in my words. "I'm just so tired, but scared to sleep."

Dropping my eyes to my feet, I scratch at a non-existent itch on the back of my neck.

Her feet shuffle, then she speaks. "Can I borrow some clothes first?"

Treading back to the bed, I drop my weight onto it and point to God's walk-in closet. "Knock yourself out. He won't notice."

A few minutes later, the bed dips, and she sits next to me, Buddha-style.

"What do you want to talk about?" she asks meekly.

"Tell me a story."

Snorting, she pushes the sleeves of a sweater much too large for her frame up her arms.

"I'm going to tell you the story of Romeo and Juliet, because I'm not sure you or the hussy who pushed me in the pool realize Romeo wasn't a womanizer."

A chuckle tightens my abs. I place a hand there and one over my eyes to cover the light from stinging my retinas.

"Is that what you think I am, a womanizer?"

Her thigh shifts, touching the side of my arm, and my heart jumps. That's pathetic. It's her clothed fucking thigh for fuck's sake, and knowing her, done one hundred percent by accident.

"I think they should call you Casanova, not Romeo."

"Okay, tell me the story of Romeo and Juliet."

A blanket covers my lower half, and I smile when she forces my head to lift and stuffs a pillow beneath it.

"It all began with two feuding families…" she begins.

"This a party of two or can anyone join?" I start awake to the sound of God's voice.

A rustling of covers and panic happening around me alerts me to Chastity jumping to her feet, hair fused like a bird's nest and creases from the blankets indented in her soft cheek.

Her voice lulled me to sleep, her presence a kind of tranquillity, her body and pulse next to mine wading me into the shadows of my mind, a safety net from the darkness of my dreams.

"Crap. It's four a.m.," she croaks, her eyes darting between God and me.

"Good night?" God smirks.

"She called me Casanova."

A pillow hits me across the head, and I chuckle. It may have only been four or five hours of sleep, but it's the most rested I've felt in forever.

"I hate you," she snaps, grabbing up her things.

"Not the usual response you receive." God snorts, kicking off his shoes.

"I hate you too, ice queen." I receive a one-finger salute before she flees the room.

My stomach protests when I go to sit up, my body hating my drinking habit and refusing to cooperate.

"God," I groan into the pillow.

"Hmmm?"

"Can you make sure she gets a cab or something? Her friend was her ride here and I doubt she's still here."

I shouldn't care how she gets home, but I do. I owe her for the dreamless sleep.

TWELVE

Twenty seconds is how long it's been since I sat down opposite the school guidance counselor. Neither of us have spoken.

I blew a tire halfway here and had to jog the rest of the way, leaving my car on the side of the road.

"Chastity," she finally says. "How has she been as a mentor for you?"

I shift in my seat to unstick my nutsack from my thigh and shake my head.

The week passed uneventfully. I managed getting to all my classes early and made some new acquaintances, but all things Elite were obsolete. Not even a murmur about the secret society—and that left me on edge. I assumed there would be an atmosphere surrounding the college, everyone waiting to see if they were going to be picked, but in reality, it really was secret and under most people's radar.

That was the whole point, but it made finding out information about them really fucking difficult.

"Rhett," Lillian coaxes, reminding me she asked me a question.

"What made you think we would be a good match?" I almost laugh, the memory of Chastity giving me the finger before she fled the room at God's party playing in my mind.

I'd seen very little of Chastity since God's party, and didn't count on changing that even if she did cause the competitor inside me to pursue her just to change her mind about me. Or too get her to talk while I slept.

Fuck it. I have more important things to worry about.

"She's well-liked on campus and knows the grounds better than most," Lillian tells me, then quirks her head to the side, studying me.

"Was there an issue?"

"Apart from Chastity hating the male species? No."

Smiling, Lillian flicks her fingers over her keyboard, typing something I can't see onto her computer.

"I'm surprised you couldn't persuade her otherwise."

Is she flirting?

"The feisty ones tend to bite. Best to leave them be." I shrug.

She changes the subject to my parents, and I spend the next twenty minutes nodding or shaking my head to her questions. I don't want to talk about why my mother isn't around right now, or that I'd seen more of Chastity last week than my dad.

"Is there anything you'd like to speak about?"

Nope.

"I'm good."

"Okay. Well, have a good day. I'll see you next week."

She doesn't follow me to the door like last time, and as I swing the door open, I almost collide with none other than Chastity.

There's a stand-off of sorts in the doorway, both refusing to apologize to the other or move out the way, even though it's clearly her clumsy ass who almost took us both out.

A sweet candy apple scent surrounds her, making my mouth water. Her eyes pierce me to the spot with defiance, the violet hints more prominent than the blue today.

Lazy and seductive, I lean in and inhale her scent before winking down at her.

"You smell real sweet today."

She narrows her eyes. "It's called a bath." She makes a point of leaning forward and sniffing at my shirt. "Ever heard of it?"

I know from running here I must stink, but that's not disgust on her pretty features. She's trying to convince herself she's not attracted to me and it's cute as hell.

I scratch at my chin, then, in a low tone, say, "Nope, can you explain it?"

"Soap, water, look it up." She tries to move around me, but I sway my body to mimic her movements just for sport.

"Isn't that where you're all naked and lathering up that creamy skin with bubbles?"

Relishing the tint to her cheeks, I brush past her, letting her move into the office, and call over my shoulder, "Thanks for the visuals, by the way, the towel over the weekend, I'll be thinking about it all day." I reel her in and watch her blow.

"You make me gag," she says, then catches her words. Her shoulders deflate, and a grin tugs high on my lips.

"Yep, sure would, sweetheart." The door slams shut, and a real chuckle resonates from my gut. Fuck, it feels good.

"You want to go to Gaspe's for lunch?" God asks, staring at his cell phone.

"You waiting on a call?"

Looking up at me for the first time since we came outside, he shakes his head.

"Just checking my fantasy football."

My own scoff almost makes me choke. "Yeah right."

A couple guys tossing a ball back and forth a couple feet away filters into my vision.

"Let's just eat on campus," I tell him, holding my hands up for the ball.

Gaspe's is my favourite place to eat. It's expensive and a thirty-minute drive away. God doesn't think about either of those things; he lives his life to a completely different tune than the rest of the world.

"Okay. I'll get them to deliver it here."

Unbelievable.

Waltzing into the parking lot, my feet skid to a halt on the gravel underfoot. No car. I forgot to arrange a ride and God fucked off after lunch. Pulling out my cell, I shoot him a text anyway.

Where you at? Need a ride.

A few seconds later, he replies.

Busy for next two hours.

Perfect.

THIRTEEN

Stacks upon stacks of books over two floors fill the space of the library. The area is airy and sparse, perfect for studying while I wait for God to pick me up.

Finding a table tucked away at the back of the room, I drop my ass in the seat and people-watch for a while. When that gets boring, I reach in my bag to pull out my books. A white envelope drops out with my name scrolled in red ink across the front.

My heart begins to thunder in my chest. Could this be it—the invitation to The Elite?

It seems too easy.

I scan the library for potential people who could have snuck it in my bag, but there's not many people here, and where I'm sitting is secluded. Anyone could have slipped this in my bag at any point today. I open it up, finding an invitation to a club inside.

What the fuck? It's just a party invite? We have an app for that, people.

My hope diminishes, and I stuff the card back in my bag and pull out my books.

Trying to ignore the not-so-subtle looks and whispers from a group of females sitting at table a good twenty feet away, I re-read the same page five times and still don't know what it says. Slamming the book closed, I sag in the chair and close my eyes. It's been over two hours, and I hit my limit at one. I need food and a shower.

"You're in my seat," a familiar feminine voice informs my almost asleep form.

Cracking an eye open, I sigh and force the other eye open. Sure enough, Chastity is standing with her arms folded over her ample chest, giving me a small glimpse of her cleavage.

"Are you sure you're not stalking me?" I ask, not moving.

"You wish, Romeo." She says Romeo as an insult, but it only makes me want to fuck her just to hear her moan it on her lips.

"This library is huge and you're harassing me for my seat?"

"My seat," she corrects.

I make a show of looking over the seat, then shrug with a satisfied smirk.

"Your name doesn't appear to be on it."

Huffing, she reaches into her bag, pulls out a book, opens it up, then drops it on the table in front of me.

A list of names, dates, and times are placed in columns down the page.

"I booked this spot from six until eight."

This has to be a joke. "You booked a seat in the library?" I mock.

"Study area, yes. This place gets real busy in the evenings—not that you'd know, it's the first time I've seen you here." She plops her bag at the foot of my chair.

"So, you've been looking for me," I surmise with a grin.

Her mouth opens and closes, then she turns on her heel and saunters off to the reception desk. I watch her speak in hushed tones, then point over at me. The guy's eyes follow her finger before he stands from behind the counter.

She flashes me a smile that says, "I've won," then walks back over to me with the library guy hot on her heels.

"I'm sorry, man, but this table is booked out from six. You'll have to move to a non-reserved spot," the guy tells me, dropping a little reserved plaque on the table.

What a brat.

"No problem. I was leaving anyway." I pack my shit up and shove to my feet. Chastity stands with her shoulders back, a victory stance.

The guy leaves us to go back to doing his job of allocating study areas. What a joke.

"You know," I say, bringing my body within breathing space of hers.

"If you took that stick out your ass, I could replace it

with my cock, that might relieve some of that tension you seem to have."

"You're disgusting." She sneers.

"Hmm or you could put those lips to use instead."

Her eyes take in every part of my face before dipping low to my crotch. "Tempting, but I'll pass. I already had Vienna sausage for lunch. One's enough for any lifetime."

"Ha!" I bark. It's natural and comes as a shock to us both. She's got jokes and that took me by surprise.

"Shhh," some guy hisses from a table where he has at least ten books cracked all at once. Nerd. Just as I'm about to tell him to shut the fuck up or I'll shut him up, God appears behind him, bending to whisper something in his ear. The guy's face blanches.

"Is he threatening him?" Chastity asks, her voice holding concern.

God marches up next to me, slapping a hand on my shoulder.

"We've got places to be," he informs me, ignoring the beauty in front of us and taking off the way he came.

"I guess that's my cue."

"Yep. Hope not to see you around." She smirks, and it does shit to me. That pretty fucking face doesn't match the bitchtude, and it's weirdly intriguing.

"You should probably stop seeking me out then." I snort, leaving her fuming in my wake.

When I get outside, God is in my car. It looks shiny and new, and I do a double take to make sure it's actually mine and not something he decided to buy on a whim.

Looking up from his cell, he says, "I had them detail it while they had it."

"You know I love you, right?" I pop the trunk and dump my bag in, then drop into the driver's seat.

"What's going on with the chick?" he asks, nodding his head toward the library.

"She's got it bad for me, just doesn't know it yet," I inform him, kicking the engine over and taking off.

"You tapped that."

"Nah. She's high maintenance as fuck. I'd have to work for it."

I've never had to work for it.

"You've never had to work for it." God jabs me in the arm, verbalising my own thoughts.

"You want to tell me where we're going?" I prompt.

Reaching into his pocket, he pulls out an envelope that matches the one I found and holds it up.

"Tell me you got one of these?"

Looking between him and the road, I jerk my head, motioning yes.

"It's just a party invite though, right?"

The galloping of my heart is back full force.

"Did you look at it?"

Briefly. I was too disappointed to inspect the fucking thing.

He holds it up, and I shrug. The party is being held at Club Envy in town.

"So what."

"Dude," he grunts, pointing to some writing at the bottom.

INVITATION TO DEADLY SINS.

"What are deadly sins?" I ask, keeping my attention on the road despite the desperate need to want to look at him and see what he's getting at.

"Don't leave me hanging, man," I bite out.

"Deadly Sins is an underground club not open to the public. You can only access it from the back of Club Envy, and my sources tell me it's an Elite ran club." He grins.

Pulling over, I cut the engine and snatch the invitation from his hand.

"Who gave you yours?" I demand, checking the thing over for any clue that this is really it, our way in.

Pulling out a vape pen, he takes a hearty pull, then fills the car with a cloud of cannabis scented vapor.

"You getting high?" I ask.

"Fuck yeah I am."

"Since when do you vape?"

Grinning he shrugs. "Some kid sold it to me."

Snatching the vape pen, I take a hit. "Woot! This is it!" I yell.

"Fuck yeah it is. Let's go get showered and shit. I have some clothes being delivered to the house. We need to look the part." He grins.

Yeah we do.

Looking good has always been something that came easy to me, but tonight I feel good too.

This is what I've wanted and been working toward, and tonight could be the night it happens for me.

God had outfits sent over that reeked of wealth and superiority. The watch hanging from my wrist costs more than my car, thanks to God's jeweler loaning me the twenty-four carat gold Rolex.

The invitation was scanned for an invisible barcode when we arrived, and unlike we assumed, we were directed to elevators taking us to a club above Envy, not below it.

God gives me an approving nod when the elevator doors open and music caresses over us like a soft wave hitting the shore. Unlike most clubs, the bass doesn't shake the room. Instead, a rhythmic pulse emits through the room, giving it a heart beat.

Bodies grind and sway on a dance floor lit up by white strobe lights, moving with the beat of the music. Glass tables that look like they were sculpted from crystal line the back walls and are occupied.

There are people of all ages enjoying themselves, and the vibe is on a level I've never experienced before.

Liquor is placed on tables by the bottle delivered by barmaids wearing tight, all black pantsuits. The fabric hugs their figures in an alluring manner without being sleazy.

God pulls out his black credit card and slides it across the bar. "Let's get wasted." He rolls his head over his shoulders and slaps my back. The bartender places drinks in front of us, but shakes his head at the credit card, pushing it back to God. Drinks are free.

Jackpot.

There are multiple private rooms throughout the club. Lights are muted inside these rooms, just a blue hue emanating from the ceiling. Alcohol stirs, intoxicating my thoughts.

Women dance around me, grinding their bodies against the hard ridges of mine.

Crooking a finger, a blonde makes a show of placing a pill on her tongue, then takes my mouth with hers, transferring the drug to me.

Our tongues dual and bodies mingle, music pulsing through me. I become part of it, my essence entering the atmosphere around me like the vapor from God's pen.

Everything feels too fucking good. More drinks are consumed, until it feels like I'm living outside my body on another plane of existence.

I'm losing myself.

My eyelids heavy. My limbs sluggish. My mind gone.

I'm floating in the emptiness of space.

FOURTEEN

Fog clouds my mind, and I hear Robbie calling to me through the haze.

"Rhett, don't forget about me."

I won't, I promise.

I promise.

I promise.

Water soaks my body as rain punishes down on me. The drops turn to acid, corroding my skin, burning me through to the bone. The sounds chop and change as my vision swims in and out, and there's a constant ringing humming through the torrent.

RING. RING. RING.

Everything is gray, dripping down the walls of my subconscious, until the images bleed into nothing and I'm pulled into consciousness.

My heartbeat is erratic and too loud in my ears. Sweat dampens my skin, saturating the sheets I find myself on.

The ringing is coming from my pocket. I'm in my bed. What the fuck? I don't even remember leaving the club. I'm shirtless, but still wearing the black jeans that look like melted black crayon against my skin. My flesh hums with an itch of a thousand tiny legs crawling under the surface. My head is groggy as fuck.

The ringing stops and immediately starts up again. I fish my cell from my pocket, and something comes with it, dropping to the floor with a clink.

Leaning over the side of the bed, I will the nausea to retreat and frown at the gold coin laying on the floor.

A skull image with writing beneath it decorates one side. Picking it up, I flick it over in my palm. The Elite Seven is embossed on the other side, and a tingle spreads throughout my body. My cell shrills in my hand, and God's name flashes on the screen. I swipe to answer his call.

"About time," his voice echoes down the line, but it's too close. My door pushes open, and God waltzes in, throwing his cell down on the bed and then catapulting himself onto the space next to me.

"I've been trying to call you for hours." He looks tired. Shades cover his eyes, but his skin is paler than usual.

"I don't even remember getting back here," I tell him. "I woke up with this." I offer him the coin, and he sits up on one elbow, taking the coin and grinning.

Handing it back to me, he burrows into his own pocket and pulls out a replica.

"Check your bedside table," he croaks.

I do, and find another invitation with coordinates and nothing else.

"We're in?" I breathe. Flopping back on the bed, a ton weight releases from my shoulders. God slaps a hand at me, catching my arm and chest. "We're in, brother."

Sighing, a real smile tugs at my lips.

"By the way, some blonde chick answered the door in her underwear. I thought she was following me back to your room, but she went into your dad's room." God shudders.

Groaning, I crawl out the bed and hit the shower. I'm sick of my dad's midlife crisis and have more important things to think about.

FIFTEEN

Wind howls through the trees, making them sound like ocean waves crashing against rock. A slither of moon shines through a break in the clouds illuminating the large brick wall standing at least twelve feet in the air, concealing the abandoned nunnery inside its concrete arms.

"You sure this is where they lead?" I ask God, snatching up the card with the directions.

"Makes sense to me. It's creepy and has a secret society vibe for sure," he says, swinging his legs out of the car and testing the iron gates.

"The driveway gates are locked, but the walkway gate is ajar." He winks, lighting up his cell phone and holding it under his chin. "You scared?" he mocks.

Leaving the car parked under a canopy of trees across

the street, I jog over to him and squeeze through the space left by the gate.

The grounds expand like black sand instead of grass under the cloak of night. About a quarter mile from where we entered is a tall, church-like building veiled in darkness, all except a lit candle flickering from the open entrance door.

"It's so cloak and dagger," God says, almost laughing.

This isn't a joke to me. He doesn't need The Elite and can take it or leave it, but I need them.

The huge, wooden door creaks under the strain and echoes through the stone corridors that greet us inside. The stone floors carry our movements, making our presence known as we descend farther inside.

We come to a circular room lit with more candles. A silhouette shadow of a male creeps up the wall like a phantom, making me search the room for the owner.

A broad figure steps out from a pillar, wide and tall, short black hair, and hard steel eyes making us out through the threshold of the space between us.

"Hey." He lifts his chin in our direction. I recognize him from Lillian's waiting area. He sees her too.

Before I have time to dwell on it, more footsteps sound from the doorway and two more males join us. I recognize one of them from campus and the other from the club last night.

There's a weighted anticipation in the air, sending a warm thrill of nervous energy coursing through my veins.

"So, do we wait here or...?" one of the guys asks while looking around the room and folding his arms over his chest. They're both athletically built like God and me.

"I've been through the entire place. This is the only

room lit up, and I found this," the broad guy with the goatee says, holding up a scroll type thing and pointing to a pew against the wall.

"It was on there." He nods his head.

"What does it say?" God asks, pulling out his cell phone turning on the flashlight, using it to search the darker parts of the room.

The place is empty. Leaves and debris litter the floor, and some graffiti has been written on the stonewalls.

"It says we have to wait for all seven of us to be here."

An awkward silence fills the room for a few seconds, until another two males join us, looking windblown and nervous. Shaggy hair hangs in one guy's green eyes. They're freaky, like fucking jewels. The other is well put-together, his hair standing up on end from his scalp.

"Hey," they say, coming into the room.

God moves his finger to each person in the room, counting us, then grins. "That's seven."

The big dude stands before us and unravels the scroll. It's a little gimmicky, but most fraternities have stupid initiations, so this is tame compared to the horror stories that come out of most campuses—and this was no sorority.

Clearing his throat, the big dude reads out, "If you stand in this room, you are witness to the chosen seven candidates. The Elite Seven." He looks up to survey his audience before continuing. "Pride. Wrath. Lust. Sloth. Gluttony. Greed. Envy."

"Do we get to choose? Because I can see me being prideful." God winks at me.

I nudge him with a, "Shhh," under my breath and continue to listen to what's being said.

"The Elite is made up of the best our school has to

offer, and you have the honor of proving yourself worthy."

The guy to my left clasps his hands together and rubs them.

"Your oath to the society will be given in action. You will perform assignments to show your obedience and dedication to The Elite. In return, you will be welcomed into a society rich, not just in wealth, but in status, influence, opportunity. You've been chosen as the crème le de crème of St. Augustine, and you will be joining the ranks of the most powerful and influential members of society."

The man flexes his jaw, and there's a spark in his eyes as he looks over us again. He's excited, just like I am. We need this.

"Above all things, we pride ourselves on candidates that will prosper long after school ends. The Elite is for life. It will become part of you. Keeping the society's secret is of utmost importance, and any indiscretion will be punishable by the full force of the society."

Taking a breath, he straightens his shoulders. "Our power is unimaginable and all that is given can be stripped away should you break your oaths."

A tense pull in the air thickens and pulses. That's a threat if I ever heard one.

"Your initiation begins with the bonding of seven. The men in this room are your brothers. The brotherhood of the seven is unbendable. You are no longer one person, you are seven."

A low whistle from the green-eyed dude punctures the air, his messy hair windswept over his head.

"I always wanted brothers." He grins, and there's something wild and untamed within it.

Ignoring his statement, the big dude continues.

"To be chosen for The Elite is of the highest honor, and for this reason, Pride is always chosen as the conduit between the initiating members and The Elite."

"Me," God lifts his chin on a whisper.

"Pride leads the seven. Prove yourselves worthy of full initiation, and you'll be welcomed into the best society the world has to offer. Your given sin reflects your abilities and personality in life, so shall it be in sin."

Blowing out a breath of anticipated air, he puts us out of the misery of suspense.

"Mason Blackwell, Pride." He looks up and gestures a hand to his chest. "That's me."

God's posture turns rigid.

"Samuel Gunner, Wrath," he reads out next, and the guy with the perfect hair steps forward.

"Rhett Masters…" *Thud.* "Lust."

Lust. Of course I'm lust. I hold a hand up to let the others know I'm Rhett.

"They don't call him Romeo for nothing," God snorts.

"Rush Dempsey, Sloth." Slouching against the back wall, one of the two who first arrived steps forward, no emotion showing on his features.

"Micah Dixon, Greed." A shoulder shrug, followed by, "I'm insatiable, what can I say?"

"Sebastian Westbrook, Envy." The guy with the feral air about him narrows his eyes on Pride, then laughs before wrapping an arm around my shoulders like we're old friends.

"I do envy you. Lust, huh? Nice," he leans in and growls in a playful manner.

"Baxter Samuel Goddard the Fifth, Gluttony."

Gluttony for God? He does love everything in excess.

I study him for a reaction, but his features are unreadable, and then Pride continues talking, distracting me.

"Good luck, and may your sins be worthy."

I'm fucking pumped. This is everything I wanted.

"There's a card," Pride announces, holding up an invitation type card like the ones we've been receiving.

God takes the three strides to Pride, and plucks it from his hand, opening it up.

"To bond your brotherhood, you will indulge in the sins of the body, in Lust."

He grins, waving the thing like a fan. Grabbing God's wrist to halt his movements, Pride takes back the card and scans his eyes over it. "There's an address. Let's go."

SIXTEEN

Silence fills the car as God swerves from lane to lane, watching in his rear-view mirror for Wrath and Envy to catch up. His pupils are the size of pinpricks, and his hand taps against the wheel incessantly.

"You feeling all right?"

His head snaps between me and the road as he nods, then laughs.

"Yeah, why?"

"You just seem more jittery than usual."

He sniffs, then shakes his head. "I just wanted to get a work out in before we did the party scene."

God is a gym freak. We both stay fit, but he took working out to a new level and had the body to prove it. He was like carved marble.

"I'm sure you'll get some working out in tonight." I

waggle my brows, and it gains me a knowing smile.

The house we pull up to is gated, a plantation home like God's, only not as big.

A security guard meets us at the entry, his bulky frame taking up the entire driver's side window. He taps his knuckles on the glass, and I lower the window.

"Tattoo or coin?" he asks.

Patting down my pockets, I rummage and pull out the coin I woke up with after the night at the club. God flicks open a tray built into the dash hidden from view. We both hold them up, and the guy takes them, inspecting their authenticity. Satisfied, he hands them back, then nods for us to go ahead.

The gates open to a short driveway leading to the impressive house. White pillars stand proud around the entire property, a grand balcony wrapping around the entire upper floor.

Parking the car, God offers me a raised brow, and I grin over at him.

"You scared?" I repeat his words back at him.

"Ask me again once we're inside. And FYI, I'm not fucking the Pride dude. He looks like a giver."

"Ha!" I bark out, holding my gut. "I don't think we have to fuck each other, but good to know you're on board with the lengths we'll have to go to get full initiation," I jest with a soft punch to his arm.

"What's funny?" Envy asks, coming up behind us, but his interest turns sharply to the house in front of us. With a low wolf whistle, he takes in all it has to offer.

"God was just letting me know how willing he is to get fucked for the brotherhood."

I wink.

"Amen to that." Envy smirks.

The others join us, and with a little apprehension in our steps, we climb the few leading to the porch.

"Ready to sell your soul for The Elite" Pride grunts, knocking his knuckles on the door.

When it opens, we're whisked into a world of pleasure and sin.

Soft music makes love to the air, setting the tone. Women, lots and lots of fuckable women, parade around in sexy underwear with seductive masks covering their faces.

"Leave your morals at the door, guys." Envy licks his lips and disappears into the sea of flesh.

This is a lot easier than I thought it was going to be.

SEVENTEEN

Drugs, whiskey, skin, sweat, moans of pleasure. Hands everywhere, lips in new places, and positions I'd never used in my life.

If all the initiation tasks are like the one a few nights ago, this shit is going to be a breeze and I'll be a full member in no time.

The corridors of St. Augustine seem richer to me now. It's odd, but I almost feel like I'm part of history—like I belong.

Shifting in class, I see everything with new eyes. I hadn't noticed him before, but looking around my economics class, I see Pride in the far back corner, his eyes already on me, assessing. He's intense, and I like that about him. He seems focused on The Elite, like me. I want to know his story. He leans into the kid sitting beside him, and when the kid grabs up his things and stands, Pride lifts his chin, then tilts his head, gesturing for me to take the seat next to him.

"This isn't musical chairs." The professor sighs as I make my way over to the vacant seat.

"Hey," I greet him, and he taps his pen to his wrist. "Nice watch."

Yeah, it is.

I still have to return this to God. Not that he gives a shit. If I wanted to keep it, he would just pay his jeweler for it. But I'm done with hand-outs. I'll earn my way.

Allowing myself a few beats to run my gaze over Pride, I take note that he doesn't wear brand clothing. His boots are military-style, built for longevity rather than fashion. He doesn't come from money like the rest of us and that intrigues me. From what I've heard of The Elite, they usually only look at members from wealthy backgrounds. Prestigious names. Maybe they are switching things up.

"Meet me at the initiation place two nights from now," Pride whispers, and then he's on his feet, leaving the class halfway through.

He made me move seats for that?

At lunch, I'm joined by Envy and Wrath. We sit in silence at first, then, like he has bees in his pants, Envy slams his hand on the wood before climbing on top of the table to plant his ass.

"We should do something tonight. Let's go out."

"I'm down." I grin, swigging my soda. "I need a high, and bonding with our brothers is what we're supposed to be doing, right?"

"Right," Envy booms. He's almost vibrating. I wouldn't be surprised if he was already high. He suddenly goes deathly still, his eyes almost darkening before my own.

Following his stare, my gaze lands on a female coming toward us. Gray eyes stare at us through a veil of brown hair, and a trim physique is showcased in a flirty summer dress. She stops at our table and hands something to Wrath. "You forgot your wallet this morning." She doesn't wait for his reply. Her eyes dart to mine and linger for a moment, then she's gone.

"Who was that?" Envy asks, getting to his feet, his gaze still following her.

"My sister, so stop checking out her ass," Wrath almost growls.

A grin tugs at my lips. That must be a nightmare for him. She's stunning. I'd bet my life on the fact that every friend he's ever had has made a pass at her—or wanted to, at the very least.

"She gave me that look." Envy announces, and I cough to cover up my laugh. He must be trying to rile up Wrath. That girl didn't even glance his way.

"If it was the look of staring at a dead man, you're right," Wrath warns, throwing a fry at him.

"Does she go here?" he asks, pushing his luck.

Jumping to his feet, Wrath grabs him in a playful headlock. They squabble while I finish my sandwich.

Releasing him, Wrath salutes us and begins to back away. "Where should we meet?"

"My house," I tell him. "I'll text the address."

"I already know where it is," Envy informs me.

Frowning, I gather my shit up and toss my trash. "Stalk much?" I joke, but his face falls like I slapped him. "I'm kidding. Meet me around nine," I reassure him.

Heading inside, my feet come up short when blonde curls brush past me in a hurry, she almost gets hit in the face with the door.

"You need to slow down," I bite out, reaching for her. She doesn't fight my grip on her wrist, but doesn't turn to face me either.

A sniffle sounds, then a soft croak. "Can you get off me now?"

Moving around her, I tuck a fallen lock behind her ear without thinking, and my heart drops.

Pretty eyes glisten with tears. Red streaks mar her soft, pale cheeks.

"What's wrong?" I ask, my voice dropping low.

I don't understand it, but there's real concern in my tone. Seeing her so distraught leaves an uneasy stirring in my gut.

"Nothing. I have a cold. Please just let me past," she begs, trying to sidestep me.

I block her exit and take her by the shoulders, moving her out of the path of the exit door and over to a secluded corner.

She huffs, but allows me to guide her before she breaks away from my hold. Dabbing her eyes, a weird snort-hiccup escapes, and then she's laughing.

"Oh my god, I'm a mess," she giggles. It's not natural, and I see real pain in her features. But I'm out of my comfort zone. My mother was always very private with her emotions apart from when *Robbie...*

"I'm sick of being me, you know? The expectation. When can I come up for air and take a breath?" She blows, pulling me back from Robbie's ghost.

I don't say anything, allowing her to vent.

"My father is a slave to his urges, but expects me to be some study machine and not let loose just one time, you know?" she continues, pacing back and forth a few steps.

She grabs the fabric of her blouse across her chest just above her tits, and thumps her hand down, drawing my eyes there.

"I just want to have a good time without worrying what's going to get back to him," she huffs, stilling her posture and taking me in.

Her observation of me is almost obscene.

Bright eyes stroke over every inch of me, lingering on my dick for far too long before roaming back up to my lips.

The scrutiny makes me squirm. It's unexpected and horny as fuck.

Taking me off guard and confusing the shit out of me, her body launches at me. Before I even realize what the hell is happening, soft, fat lips crush to mine, hands find their way into my hair, and soft tits press against my chest as her warm tongue slips into my mouth.

It's rushed, rough, inexperienced, and fucking perfection.

Her sweet apple blossom scent wraps its arms around me, cocooning me in the moment. I wrap her in my embrace and back her against the wall, devouring her mouth, nibbling and caressing. My dick hardens, demanding I push against her. Suddenly, her body stiffens beneath mine, and her hands drop to my shoulders, pushing me.

I pull away, dizzy with lust. I breathe deep, ready to fuck her right here in the corridor.

Red swollen lips tremble, and wild, sex-crazed eyes dance with trepidation.

"I'm sorry. Oh my god, what am I doing?" she all but squeals. "This was…" She frowns.

"Horny as hell?" I offer.

"A mistake." She focuses those blues on me.

"A beautiful mistake," I counter with a swipe of my tongue across my lips.

"You better not tell a soul about this. Promise me."

"What?"

"Promise me?" she says, more urgent.

"Who would care?" I laugh, but her eyes narrow to slits.

"I don't want to be one of your conquests," she growls before crossing her arms and storming off.

Who the fuck would I tell?

EIGHTEEN

Moans, fake and high-pitched, greet me when I get home. The naked form of a female is laid out on the study room floor on what looks like a tarp.

What the actual fuck?

I move closer, then halt. My dad is standing above her, hovering at her head, holding his dick. He begins pissing on her as she pants and rubs it in like its nectar from the gods.

What the fucking hell? Gross. He's always seemed so uptight and vanilla. I can't un-see this shit. He better not have done this kinky shit to my saint of a mother, the fucking pervert.

"I have people coming over, so if you could wrap that up, or at least close a fucking door, that will be great." I grunt, rolling my eyes. I drop my keys on the counter, ignoring the woman squealing and slipping as she tries to get up.

It would be fucking comical if this weren't our family home and that wasn't once my mom's study.

His midlife crisis is getting old.

I grab a cartoon of juice and throw my ass onto the couch in the living room, watching through the doorway as the woman who looks like his old secretary throws on her clothes and hurries to leave.

Wearing only a pair of low-rise slacks, my old man saunters into the living room and stands facing me, lines creasing his eyes and forehead. I hate how much he reminds me of me. I don't want to be anything like him.

Hands go to his hips to intimidate. Prick.

"We need to talk."

I sit forward, resting my arms on my knees.

"About you fucking whores in my mother's house?"

"My house," he barks.

He's pathetic. He got the house in the divorce, but this will always be my mother's house.

"You'll get used to seeing Melissa around here. She's not a fling, and certainly not a whore."

Melissa. That was his fucking secretary.

"If you say so," I spit out, getting to my feet.

Raging forward, his hand swipes out fast, catching the carton and sending it flying across the room.

"You will learn respect, Rhett. I'm sick of your disrespectful bullshit," he seethes.

Me disrespectful? He must be fucking high to accuse anyone of that when he's a disgrace. The only name being whispered about and doing damage to our family reputation is his.

Fucking sluts half his age and cheating with his secretary.

He gives no fucks about my mother, me, or the memory of his son. Not once has he spoken about Robbie or been to his grave. I wonder if he even thinks about him. Does Robbie visit him when he closes his eyes like he does me?

"Are you even listening to me?"

No.

"I give respect to people I R.E.S.P.E.C.T." My tone is grinding, blood rushes through my veins like a raging current.

I see it coming, but it's too fast on impact for me to prevent it. The fist hits my jaw, sending my head snapping to the side.

It's not the first time he's hit me, just the first time since I've been as big as him, and the first time with a closed fist.

My muscles coil as my mind explodes like a ticking time bomb reaching zero. I charge him.

Shock registers in his eyes before my shoulder collides with his midsection, taking him down.

We hit the wood floor hard, making the air whoosh out of him. I rise to rain down a flurry of blows, but stop short when his body doesn't move.

His eyes closed...and just fucking nothing.

What the fuck is this shit?

Pushing myself off him, I back away, searching his form for life.

What the hell happened? My pulse gallops uncontrollably, and then my stomach rolls.

A red liquid pool seeps from under his head like

spilled wine.

Oh fuck. Oh fuck. Oh fuck.

This can't be happening.

How? I didn't even hit him.

The blood oozes, and the image of it evokes fear deep in my soul. I killed him.

Stirring in my gut intensifies, and I rush to the toilet to expel my lunch.

I killed him.

I killed him.

Fuck.

Fuck.

With shaky hands, I pull out my cell phone and call the only person I can rely on.

"I'm not late. You said nine," he shouts out before I can say anything.

"I need you to come now." My voice sounds hoarse to my own ears.

"What? You sound weird."

"Come now. Something happened. I need you to come now."

Voices chatter through the receiver. He's not alone.

Panic washes over me like a damp mist.

"Who are you with?"

"Rush."

"Who?"

"Sloth, dumbass," he says, irritation in his response. He hates me calling everyone by their sin name in favor of their given names.

"We're on our way." He ends the call before I can tell him to come alone.

Fuck.

Scenarios of the consequences pulse through my head.

Accidental death. My life goes on.

Self-defense. My life goes on.

Murder charges. I go to prison until I'm decrepit, forgotten about, and left to rot.

I'm pacing the floor of the foyer when God and Sloth arrive. They waltz straight in, and I berate myself for not locking the damn door. Anyone could have walked in here, and then my choices would be out of my control.

"Lock the door," I urge, receiving frowns from them both.

"I called the others. They're all on the way," God tells me without moving to lock the door.

"Why the fuck would you do that?" I bark in alarm.

Walking toward me, God places his hands on my shoulders, making me stare at him.

"You're freaking me out. You having a bad trip?"

I'm not high. Fuck, I wish I was.

"I killed him," I vomit out.

Silence. Tick. Tick. Tick.

"I'm sorry?" Sloth says, stepping forward and turning his face to hear me better. "What did he just say?"

A knuckle tap sounds at the front door, and Pride joins us, followed by the others a few seconds later.

Not even a full week we've been bonded, and now they all stand in my house, witnesses to murder.

I murdered my dad.

My throat seizes, and I choke, coughing into a frenzy.

"What's going on?" I recognize Pride's baritone.

God holds me up, patting my back. "Are you all right?"

Typical of him to be concerned with my wellbeing and not the fact that I told him I killed someone.

"Oh fuck," someone barks, and all attention slides to whoever ventured into the living room.

I follow them as they descend into the space where my dad lays dead on the floor.

"Okay," God says, nodding his head and looking between the body and me.

Pride points to my chin, then down to my dad. "He do that to you?"

Why aren't any of them freaking out? I reach up to the bruise blossoming there.

Sloth looks to be the only one taking this for what it is. They're all involved with murder. He's solemn, his legs giving out and all but falling on to the couch.

"This is bad," he mumbles.

"He hit me, and I just took him down. I didn't…I don't…"

"Breathe," Greed tells me, nodding. "You're not alone in this."

"We'll get rid of the body." Envy shrugs a shoulder, like he's talking about moving a couch. "The swamp. Gators will take care of it."

"It's not an it. It's a fucking person. Christ," Wrath grinds out, sifting a hand through his hair.

"No, Envy is right. We protect our brother. We get rid of the evidence," Pride pipes up.

"What about when someone asks where the fuck he is?" Wrath demands.

"He's fucking every floosy in this town. Rhett says he

went off with some woman. No one will think otherwise," God snorts.

"We worry about that after. For now, we need to get rid of him," Envy says.

Can I do this? Let gators eat his body?

"There's tarp in the study," I announce, pointing in that direction.

Pride follows my line of sight. "Do we want to know why there's tarp in your study?"

"No, you really don't. It has his piss on it, so be careful picking it up."

Curious stares all aim at me.

"Golden shower."

In and out, in and out. I focus on my breathing as Envy and Pride wrap my dad in the tarp used for his sex games. I bet he never expected this outcome when he bought it for their perversions.

"What car do we use?" Wrath asks, patroling around the room.

"His," I offer up. "It's in the garage. No one will see us loading his body into it."

"Good." Pride nods his head manically.

"I'll stay and clean up the blood," Wrath offers. "I'll help with that, watch to make sure he gets it all," Sloth says without moving. Wrath marches out of the room. Cupboards opening and closing sound from the kitchen.

"The rest of us will dispose of the body," Pride commands.

Dispose of the body.

Dispose of the body.

Dispose of the body.

Rushing out of the room, I sprint up the stairs to vomit where they can't hear me.

Trapped like sardines in the car, I feel like I'm floating above the scene and not actually a part of it. It's surreal, If I couldn't feel an elbow in my ribcage and have no sign of Robbie, I'd swear I was dreaming.

Night has claimed the sky, giving us the cloak of darkness we need.

Pride drives while God directs him to some marshlands beyond God's property line. He told us they didn't buy it because it's uninhabitable and no one goes there so it was pointless. It's a perfect dumping ground for serial killers.

Or teen boys playing grown men.

"Thank you," I blurt out from the backseat. I don't need to elaborate. They all know what I'm thankful for. They're risking their entire futures for me: a stranger.

"We're a brotherhood," Pride grunts, and silence follows.

Turning onto a dirt road that becomes just dirt and shrubbery after a minute, Pride pulls the car to a stop.

"The car won't go much farther. We can't risk it getting stuck."

"We can walk the rest of the way," Envy says, almost too normal. He throws the door open and jumps out of the car like we're on a road trip.

Greed's eyes clash with mine, his brow raised at Envy's upbeat attitude in the situation,

We crowd the trunk like we don't know if the body is still going to actually be there, all praying we dreamed this night. But it's not a dream. His body is exactly where it was placed.

Reaching in, Pride hoofs it over his shoulder like it's weightless. Not even a grunt. He's a beast.

"Let's get this done," he grumbles, taking off through the trees.

"Not what I thought we'd be doing tonight." God slaps a hand on my back.

Before I can answer, Pride jumps back, tossing the tarp-wrapped body to the ground with a thud. It rolls across the ground, unravelling, and my father's body springs free—and moves.

He's fucking moving.

With sluggish movements he lifts up onto his knees, groaning in pain. Shit.

"What the hell?" He groans lifting himself up further and making it to his feet. Holding a hand to the back of his head he winces and checks his palm for blood.

I need to pick my jaw up that's slack and say something but words won't form past the stone in my throat.

Swaying on unsteady feet he looks around until he sees me. Blinking as if to clear his thoughts he groans out. "What's going on, Rhett?"

Fuck. Fuck. Fuck.

Pride turns his angry glare on me. "Did you check him for a fucking pulse?"

Well, shit.

"I...erm..."

"Did anyone?" Pride fumes.

A cackle of laughter roars through the air, and Envy bends over to slap at his knee.

"Classic." He swipes tears from his eyes. "I've got this," he finishes. Pulling a blade from a strap on his ankle, he waltzes toward my dad, making him stammer backwards and trip on the uneven terrain in fear of his life.

I'm solidified, the roots of the wilderness binding me to my spot as heat flushes up my spine and sprouts spores all over my body.

He's not dead.

"Dude," God snaps at Envy.

Pride stops his advance with a tug on his arm and a shake of his head.

"What?" Envy asks, confused.

"Dude?" God says again, shaking his head. "Put the knife away."

"Where the fuck did you get the knife?" Greed screws his face up, judging Envy's crazy.

"Rhett, what's going on?" my dad asks, a quake in his voice. Bugs bite at all our skin, and the whispering of the trees makes the place feel haunted as fuck. I inhale the first real breath since taking his ass down earlier tonight. Sucking at the air to fill my lungs, it feels like I've been in a choke hold, the devil breathing down my neck, hell climbing into my soul.

"You hit me," I say, unsure what the hell is happening myself. I thought he was dead. In my panic, I didn't even check his pulse.

"My head hurts," he groans.

"You fell and hit your head," God tells him.

"Why are we out here, and who are these people?" he questions, wary.

Stepping forward, Pride towers over my dad's hunched over form, his build alone intimidating as shit. "We're his brothers, and we're willing to do whatever necessary to protect him, and his future, even if that means you gotta lose yours," Pride warns, his threat razor sharp.

"What happened tonight?" God asks him. The other's crowd in around him like serpents ready to strike.

Stuttering and gasping for air, my dad scans the pack surrounding him and nods in understanding. "I fell and hit my head. Rhett took me to hospital. That's it."

"That's it," Pride repeats, the warning as loud as a lion's roar.

NINETEEN

God's always had my back, but knowing the lengths others are willing to go for me gives me a sense of invincibility and the feeling of family I've been missing lately.

My dad has given me a wide berth since that night. And the bond between the seven of us feels like a lifetime of friendships, not a week.

Pride is already at the convent when I arrive. Lit candles surround him as he reads over a card in his hands.

"Just us?" he asks as I make my presence known.

"God," I call out, and my best friend steps out from behind the door.

Standing, Pride nods and holds the card between his finger and thumb.

"I've been given your task." His lips slice into a thin line.

Anticipation shudders through me. This is it—what it's going to cost for my membership.

"You want me to read it out loud, or…?" I take the card from his hand and swallow.

"You should know," he says, serious and firm.

"The coin given to you by The Elite offers you one trade or future favor. If you cash it in, to forfeit your task, you won't be given a choice of the second task chosen for you. You will need to follow it through or be expelled as a candidate. Using your coin now leaves you no future favors, shall you ever need something not given freely by The Elite," he urges with a firm grip to my shoulder. "Think carefully about this choice. You only get one."

"Noted." I open the card and read the ink elegantly swirled on the paper.

Lust,

Your task is sin of the flesh.

Miss. C. Griffins.

Academic protégé.

Heir to her family fortune.

Daughter to the Dean of St. Augustine.

Seduce the forbidden fruit.

Document the sin.

Bribery shall The Elite ever need it.

It's signed with the stamp, same logo as on the coin.

"She sounds like a perfect candidate for The Elite," I scoff.

"Maybe she was." Pride quirks a brow, a wicked grin curling up his lip.

Hands bare down on my shoulders from behind,

God squeezing. "Romeo, Romeo," he mocks in a playful manner.

Taking the card from my hand, Pride holds it up. "You got it?"

"Easy," I offer him a grin of my own, but it's all bravado. Seducing women out of their panties isn't an issue for me, I've been a pro at it ever since my balls dropped, but filming her without her knowledge and giving it over so fuck knows how many people can view it doesn't sit well with me.

I'm an asshole, but that much of one?

Pulling a silver lighter from his pocket, Pride lights the card, the flame taking hold, consuming my task.

Dropping it to the floor, we all watch transfixed as the amber flame dies out and ash is the only thing remaining.

Now, all I need to do is find out who Miss Griffin is.

Arriving back at the house, I'm met on the driveway by an electrician's truck and my dad hurrying out the house.

"You'll need to order dinner in," he tells me, rushing to his car.

"What's with the workmen?" I call after him.

"That's your best friend's doing, not mine," he calls back.

God offers me a wicked smile and lets himself into the house, taking the stairs two at a time.

I follow him to my room and find him in the attached bathroom.

"What the…?"

The light in my bathroom is now a black light.

"You're going to want to see your tattoo once you smash this task," he informs me.

"The tattoos only show under these lights. It's why I've

never seen my dads."

I snort. "That, and his is probably lost in his rolls," I jest.

Ignoring my insult, he says, "At the club, I saw one on the thigh of a woman." He waggles his eyebrows.

"Do you think it's wrong to film me fucking her?" I ask, changing the subject and finally letting some of my apprehension filter out.

"Since when do you have morals?" He jabs me in the arm. "You'll get this done in no time. Don't let yourself think about her, this is about you."

About me.

"No matter what the task is, remember," he reminds me of my own words.

"Right. We have to do this," I say, not just to him, but to myself.

"No matter what," I reaffirm.

Following him back downstairs, he rummages through our cupboards, coming up empty.

"Dude, where's the fucking food?"

Cocking a brow, I pull my cell phone out. "Chill, Gluttony, I'll order some pizza."

Two hours later, I've eaten two thirds of the pizza and a liter of soda, and God hasn't touched his. Instead, he's waiting not so patiently for me to get ready to go racing with him.

He's going to be pissed when I bail. I just want to get high and try to crash.

TWENTY

God is absent from campus again. My text from him this morning was at four a.m. and he was still out.

God: Want to get high?

I was already high and tossing and turning in my sweat-drenched sheets.

Dreams of Robbie were mixed with dreams of an unknown female crying. A video was spread through campus of her being fucked in every orifice by me.

My soul was heavy. Maybe this chick will turn out to be a fucking cunt and then I won't feel so bad.

Lies.

Pride is in the waiting area when I reach the counselor's room. It's going to be twice as hard to talk to her now knowing I have to fuck her stepchild.

Intrigue prickles my thoughts as to why Pride has to

see her. Has he lost someone like me?

"What's up?" he acknowledges me.

"You have an appointment?" I ask, checking the clock. It's just ticking on ten, which is when my appointment starts.

He shakes his head no, then holds up a folder, but doesn't elaborate on what's in it.

"I have to drop these off."

The door opens, and Lillian appears, well put-together and fresh. Her hair is pulled so tight, it lifts her eyes to almost slits.

"Rhett. Go on inside," she orders, stepping out from her office and going to Pride.

Yes, ma'am.

Closing the door behind me, I hit a fog wall of stuffy air. Moving over to her window, I nudge the thing open. The weather is humid as hell, like being in a steam room. You can taste peoples' sweat in the corridors, it's so sticky.

My interest moves to her shelves dominating the back wall. Books, files, pictures. My heart stammers when my fingers trace over a family photo of Lillian, the dean, and none other than Chastity.

Shit.

The opening of the door alerts me to Lillian's arrival. She catches me with the picture in my hand and raises one of her perfectly shaped brows.

"Chastity," I say, pointing to the image like an idiot.

"Yes," she confirms, taking the picture from my hand and placing it back on the shelf.

How have I not noticed it until now?

"She's my stepdaughter, hence her knowing her way around the campus as well as she does." She smiles.

"I have to go," I tell her, hiking my bag up my shoulder and turning on my heel, fleeing her room.

Chastity is who I have to seduce and film?

This just got a lot more complicated. For one, she doesn't even like me, and two, I know her, sort of. It's immoral and sleazy. It's…the price.

"Hey."

Fuck, speak of the devil.

"Hey," I mimic, looking around the corridor at anyone but her.

"Look, I want to apologize for what happened the other day." She sighs, and it furrows *my* brow. Why the hell is she sorry? I was the one who didn't let her run away to cry and then took advantage of her in crisis.

"Really?" I ask, apprehension coloring my tone.

"I was a mess and put that on you, and that's not who I am. I acted out and made a mistake, but you haven't made a point of using it against me and no one has mentioned it, so…" she says, pushing her glasses up her nose.

I've been too busy to use it against her, and who would I tell? Oh, of course, with her being the dean's daughter, she's no doubt been used in the past for that very reason.

"Rhett, I'm apologizing." Her voice is firm, and a little peeved that I'm staring into space and not taking her words as serious as she appears to.

"Thanks."

I guess.

Silence.

She looks at her shoes, then back up at me. Is that nerves making her jittery?

"Maggie is having a party this weekend. It would be good to see you there, if you want…to go…you don't have to…I don't really care either way…"

"I'll be there," I blurt, stopping her rambling. Why the fuck is she making this easy for me?

"As friends," she states. "Be good to see a friend there…friendly face…familiar…"

"Right," I stop her again. "Who doesn't need more friends?" I smile.

Tucking her hair behind her ear, she bounces on her tiptoes and bites her lips.

"Right. Okay. Great."

She walks around me, and I turn to watch her flee. She stops a couple feet away, and turns back to me. "Oh, you may need the address."

I don't tell her it will be on the party app because this flustered Chastity is the girl who bumped into me on the first day of class. I like this side of her.

"Phone?" She holds her hand out and waits for me to place my cell in her palm.

She flits her thumbs over the keypad and hands it back.

"I programmed my number in and texted myself so I have your number. I'll text over the address. It's easier that way." She nods her head, biting back down on the fat bottom lip. A red rouge sprouts over her cheeks and crawls down her neck.

"Thanks," I say, knowing she just wanted my number. I've used that same method more times than I can count.

I sense the body creep up before Chastity's eyes move to the shadow behind me.

She places her hands in the pocket of her jacket and turns on her heel without turning back this time.

"By the look she was giving you, I'd say you're already

halfway to completing your task," Pride teases.

So, he knows exactly who she is then. Schooling my features, I turn to face him and smirk. "What can I say? It's in my DNA."

We fall in step, heading toward the food court.

"Speaking of your DNA, how has your dad been?"

He's been too scared to say shit to me. Seeing how easy it would be for me to get rid of him spooked the hell out of him.

"Good," is all I say.

The following days pass fast, and as if the world knows what my task is and wants to make it easy on me, destiny keeps placing Chastity in my path.

I parked next to her this morning without realizing it was her car. She was in three of my classes today and within breathing space of my lungs. Her scent surrounded me, beckoning, teasing, daring me to take a bite of her delicious innocence.

As if she's drawn to me by a magnetic pull, her eyes drift to me more than they should.

She texted me the address for her best friend's party. And then sent follow up random texts that made no sense throughout the day.

"What can be both healing and poisonous?"

"The glare of what reveals the others?"

I'm not sure if she's sending them to the wrong number or she's a spammer. Either way, they made no sense.

Closing my book, I stumble into the corridor and

wipe sweat off my brow. Running on zero sleep and coming down from my mom's old anxiety medication she left when she abandoned us, has left my body lethargic. I need a sugary drink to perk me up.

Rushing over to a vending machine, I pat down my pockets, then slap the glass when there's only a slot for cards, which I need to remember to ask my old man for. I think he will revaluate my need for a credit card after I nearly inherited everything he has last week.

"Here" Pride slides his card into the machine. I punch the button for a soda and stuff a twenty into Prides jacket pocket.

"That was an expensive drink."

"And it didn't even get me laid." I wink.

Waving a bye over my shoulder as I head for the exit. Pushing out the door and into the stuffy air I groan when the smog hits me like a sweat bath. When it's not raining here the air is too thick, I hate it.

When I finally make it to my car, there's a cute blonde leaning against it.

"Chastity," I greet her.

She's making this too damn easy. I thought she was going to be a challenge, but it appears not spreading rumors about her kissing me was enough to warrant me friendship status.

How fucked up have people been to her in the past?

"Here." She hands me a wrapped present. Twine binds the brown paper wrapped around something that feels like a book. I'm not sure what to say.

"Thanks," I say, raising a brow.

She laughs and rolls her eyes. "Relax, it's not a snake in a box."

"That's pretty dark," I say, repeating her words.

Shaking her head, she goes to her own car, and calls out, "It's for research—and to help you sleep."

Dropping the package on my bed, I snap the twine and unravel the paper.

A rich sound ricochets from my chest. Laughter. Authentic and deep.

Romeo and Juliet by William Shakespeare.

I open the book, and a USB falls out. What are the chances this is a sex tape and she's done my task for me?

Reaching for my laptop, I plug in the stick and lay back on the bed.

"Romeo and Juliet narrated by Chastity Griffin, for Rhett Masters, to teach him he's far from a Romeo." The voice billows from the speakers into the room, enveloping me.

Ha. She's still got her feisty edge.

Her voice caresses the words, blanketing me in a soothing melody, and my eyes close to submerge myself in the world of Capulets and Montagues.

I sleep a full eight hours, and it almost brings tears to my eyes. No rain. No voices. No Robbie. Just her.

No drugs to quiet my mind. Just her.

TWENTY-ONE

Wrath, Envy, and Pride join me for Maggie's party, but I'm not sure how long they will last. Unlike most college parties, this one doesn't have people spilling onto the front lawn or music vibrating the foundations. A sweet melody of blues filters through the room, and everyone is dressed in the twenties attire. There was no alert for this party or text from Chastity letting me know there was a theme.

There are maybe thirty people here, and by the way they talk animatedly, they appear to all know each other.

Envy gives me the stink eye, and Pride tries to hold in his amusement.

"Things we do for ass." Wrath flexes his jaw and snatches up a drink from a guy wearing a white suit and gangster hat. "Beat it," Envy hisses at him when he stops to challenge his drink being taken.

"Relax. Let's give it thirty minutes," Pride says, studying the room.

"Twenty," Envy and Wrath say in unison.

My phone beeps with a text message.

Chastity: So sorry. Can't make it. Stuck at the house. Another time.

Unbelievable.

Waving my phone up, I turn for the exit. "How about one minute."

"Oh, Romeo, get stood up?" Envy hoots.

"She's on house arrest."

"So break her out." Envy grins mischievously.

"Anyone know where the dean lives?" I huff, only half joking.

We pile into Pride's car and take off toward town.

"I know where he lives," Envy chirps.

Of course he does.

Mist coats the road as night descends, bringing with it a chill to the air.

"Take a right here, then the second left," Envy directs.

We pull down a road with tall, modern houses—nothing like I'd expect her to live in. "That one."

"Do we want to know how you know this?" Wrath shivers, the nip in the air closing in.

"I think his wife is fit."

All heads swivel judgingly toward him.

Holding up his hands, he wrinkles his forehead. "Chill out. I was walking past one night on my way to a friend's house and saw her in the window. Jeez."

Pride slows the car to a stop and I get out, raking my

eyes over the structure.

One of the windows on the first floor is open. The curtains billow in the gentle breeze, giving us glimpses of a pink room and Chastity pacing while she reads from a book in her hand.

"Good luck," Wrath calls from the car before they take off, wheels squealing and kicking up dirt, leaving me on the side of the road. Motherfuckers. Walking home is going to suck.

Giving my attention back to the window, I find Chastity staring at me through the gap, her eyes wide and jaw slack.

She disappears, then reappears, typing something on her phone.

A second later, mine beeps.

Chastity: What are you doing here? My father will freak if he sees you."

Me: Maggie's was a snoozefest. Only person there I wanted to see didn't show.

I wave my hand to get her to come down and talk to me, but she shakes her head vehemently.

Chastity: My dad is mad at me and will ground me for life.

I want to remind her she's eighteen, but like with my own father, they have pull over us with money and a roof over our heads.

Me: I'll come up.

I can sense her panic before I see it on her pale face.

Pointing to a flower trellis attached to the side of her house, I move to it and give it a shake. It wobbles slightly, but should be okay.

I make it up after two near misses, the lattice grill

snapping underfoot. The roof juts out, bordering the first floor, giving me easy access to get to her window.

She's shaking and searching the grounds as she pokes nearly half her body out the window.

"Hey," I say, breathing heavy and wiping dirt off my hands.

"You're insane," she pants.

"Or romantic." I quirk a brow.

Snorting, she says, "Yes, very Romeo of you."

As I move toward her, my foot slips on moss, my stomach dips.

I reach out for purchase of her windowsill, but miss.

Her arms flail to reach for me, but it's too late. I slip, meeting air, then land on her front lawn with a heavy thud.

My ribs roar, flaring in pain as I land directly on my side.

"Motherfucker," I croak.

The porch lights flick on, and I hear movement.

Getting hastily to my feet, I make for the brush surrounding the property and dive for cover as the door opens.

"Hello?" a deep baritone barks.

Just when I think I've gotten away with it and he retreats, my phone beeps.

"Who's there?" he shouts.

I take off on crouched knees through the thicket of bush, the twigs and debris scratching holes into my jeans. If it didn't hurt like a son of a bitch, this shit would be hilarious—something I'm definitely not sharing with the group.

When silence is my only company, I stand, brush

myself off, and tug my phone out.

Chastity: Romeo, Romeo, where art thou?

Me:_Parting is such sweet sorrow that I shall say goodnight till it be morrow.

Chastity: You've been reading.

Me: Listening. It's the only thing that helps me sleep. I've been meaning to thank you for that.

Chastity: So thank me.

Me: I will in person.

Chastity: How about tomorrow night?

Me: Name the place.

Chastity: Meet me at the end of my street. Eight o'clock.

Me: Done.

Chastity: Goodnight, Rhett Masters.

Me: Goodnight, Chastity Griffin.

TWENTY-TWO

Ignoring the incoming call from God, I slip my car into park at the end of Chastity's street and get out.

Last night, I slept like a baby. No drugs needed. This audio reading from Chastity has been a revelation.

Her voice lulls me into a state of calm.

She's doing things to me, and I don't know how this is all going to play out once my part is completed.

Guilt eats away at me when I see her bounding toward me.

She's not like most girls our age. She has the wisdom beyond her years, but she's been sheltered, and it shows.

I bet she's a fucking virgin—and that makes my task ten times fucking worse.

You'd think with how powerful The Elite is, the dean would be someone within their ranks, but no, so they resort to shitty tactics for future needs.

"Hey, you came," she says, breathless from the jog down to me.

"Of course. Did you think I wouldn't?" I smirk.

A small lift of her shoulders tells me the answer.

Gesturing to the car, I ask, "Where to, my lady?"

Shaking her head, she wraps her cardigan over her small frame and jerks her chin toward the road.

"There's a park just through there. Let's walk."

I haven't hung around in a park since I was seven, but this girl is different and I need to embrace that if I have intentions of seducing her.

Do you have those intensions? My subconscious asks, I silent the voices by asking her questions.

"So, Mrs. Griffin, huh? Is it hard having people know the guidance counselor and dean are your parents?"

"She's not my parent." She shakes her head, looking between the road and me.

Sore subject?

"Oh I'm sorry…"

"No, it's fine, it's just, she's my dads wife, that's it. His choice not mine."

Nodding my head in understanding I ask.

"Are you an only child?"

Nodding her head causes her hair to fall into her face, and I ache to slip it behind her ear and stroke her cheek, take her mouth with mine.

"Yes. My mother died in childbirth." A pained grimace takes over her pretty features.

That's rough.

"How about you?" she asks innocently enough, but the pain slashes into me nonetheless.

Her startled eyes grow impossibly large, and almost violently, she reaches for me and pulls me into her body.

"I'm so sorry," she chokes out. "I don't know why I asked when I already know. It was insensitive and foolish, an accident… I wouldn't try to hurt you—or anyone—like that," she rambles, and I pull free and smile down at her to ease her tension.

Slipping my fingers into her hair, I finally tuck it behind her ear, then let the pad of my thumb caress her cheek.

"It's okay. Honestly, don't worry about it." After a silent pause, we continue walking.

"I googled you," she says, flicking her embarrassed gaze to mine, halting our movements.

"That's how I know about…" she gulps, fidgeting with an invisible thread on her cardigan, "your brother."

The usual constricting pain grips my heart in a vice at the mention of Robbie.

"I'm so sorry. That must have been…"

"Death," I rasp. "Like death," I add, breathing air into my broken lungs. "It felt like I died with him."

"But you didn't," she whispers, almost asking me the question instead of making a statement.

A humorless laugh rattles my chest. "What's that saying? What doesn't kill you only makes you wish it did?" I vomit my truth out, surprising us both with my forthcoming emotions.

"You always seem so full of life, happy…"

Grief, borrowed from our shared experiences, fills her eyes.

"That's just the mask, I'm drowning, but with a smile on my face knowing I can't be saved," I confess, letting myself open up to her.

"That must be exhausting." She murmurs, lines creasing her forehead.

It fucking is exhausting.

My mind is like a carousel going around in circles. Different scenarios bring different outcomes, but it can't be changed, no matter how much I will it. I'm telling myself these truths as much as I'm telling her.

"My world's a mess right now, of regret and sorrow." I almost choke on the last word, grief filling me up from the tips of my toes to the roots of my hair, my world quaking beneath me, threatening to consume all I am.

Her warm hand slips into mine, squeezing, reassuring, comforting. The ground settles and I can breathe.

"You're right here," she says in almost a whisper. Her other hand comes to rest on my chest where my heart beats slow beneath it's shelter.

"You're not allowed to die with him. You have to live for you both."

My posture sags and my head leans forward, too heavy for my shoulders.

"I promised myself that's what I'd do for my mom," she says, vulnerability shaking her voice.

"She wouldn't want me to let the cruelty of fate stop me from living my best life, so like a ghost attached to my heart, she's with me. It beats for us both. We're both living."

Reaching my hand up without thought, I rest it against her own heartbeat. She doesn't pull away or falter. This isn't about me copping a feel—it's two people sharing pain, learning to live through it, and finding a connection to help us keep living, keep breathing, keep standing, one foot in front of the other, until it stops hurting.

Da-dum. Da-dum. Da-dum.

"Come on." She smiles, breaking the contact and recommencing our path to her destination. I haven't talked to anyone about Robbie, and it helps—it really fucking helps.

We walk in silence for a few beats, but it's not uncomfortable, it just is.

Nudging me toward a treeline, she turns to venture through the thicket.

"Are you going to lure me in there and then have your way with me?" I drawl.

Slapping me playfully, she pushes me farther into the trees, the dirt caking our boots.

"If you mean kicking your ass, then maybe."

"I might be into sadism," I snigger out, walking farther into no man's land.

"I think you'll find that's a masochist," she points out, dodging tufts of growth.

Just when I'm about to ask her what the difference is, the trees open up and an old park emerges in a clearing. The terrain is covered in undergrowth, the framework of the slide and swing rusted by years of being unused. It's spooky and kind of beautiful all in the same breath.

"Be careful of snakes," she tells me, her southern drawl more potent when she talks about the dangers.

"Why is this here?" I ask, taking her hand to help her manoeuvre over some fallen branches.

"It was part of the Miller's property in the late fifties. They died over two decades ago and their land was abandoned. This part was claimed back by nature. The house was vandalised and eventually torn down when a girl claimed she was attacked and taken there."

Frowning, I sit on the swing next to her and try to move it. It protests loudly, but eventually begins to move, raining down orange on my head.

"That got dark," I state, and she smiles, white teeth on display.

"Are you not scared to come here?" I ask, searching the woods as the sun sets. Everything drops in temperature, making the place twice as creepy as before.

"Why would I be? What are the odds of us both being serial killers?" she asks, narrowing her eyes on me.

It takes a few seconds, but we both burst into a fit of laughter.

I like her more and fucking more.

"Seriously, though, don't come here on your own," I warn, my protectiveness spiking, surprising us both.

"I won't, I promise. This can be our place."

Our place. I like that.

We talk for hours, about nothing, about everything, in the blue light from the full moon above. Soon, I know our night will come to an end, but I don't want it to.

It's so peaceful here away from the expectation and stress of school. Away from the reputation and rumors.

"Why are nice girls always attracted to bad boys?" she asks on the walk back to my car.

"Am I a bad boy?" I raise a challenging brow.

"The question you should be asking is, am I a good girl?" she counters as we slow to a stop by my car.

"Are you?"

The air between us is palpable. My skin hums with electricity as she closes the space between us. Looking up into my eyes, she murmurs, "I don't want to be, when

I'm around you."

Her lips hover so fucking close, but so far. Cupping her face, I push my lips to hers, chaste and sweet, before backing away. "Then let me be the good one for both of us," I tell her, ignoring the straining of my cock and the pulsing of my blood screaming at me like a bloodthirsty night crawler wanting to devour her whole.

She touches a finger to her lips, her eyes heavy and cheeks flushed.

"Goodnight, Rhett Masters."

"Goodnight, Chastity Griffin."

I watch her walk to her house and disappear from view before I release the breath I'd been holding and brace my arms against the roof of my car to steady my heartbeat.

I've honestly never felt this kind of need before, and of all people, it had to be with her.

I'm fucked.

TWENTY-THREE

The days pass in a haze of all things Chastity. She's become my addiction, occupying my every thought. At school, she offers me coy smiles, followed by texts referencing Romeo and Juliet quotes or trivia.

Usually, this kind of shit would have me running for the hills, but not with her.

I've held off doing anything with her but a peck on her lips here and there, but there's tension so thick between us, I'm sure the atmosphere around us shimmers with big signs stating how bad we want to fuck each other.

"Rhett, please put your phone away for a few seconds," my dad says, nervousness catching in his voice.

He's scared of me—no, not of me, of what I'm capable of. He knows I'm part of The Elite, or will be, because God isn't subtle when talking about it when he's here, which is less and less as of late. It's my fault. I've been too preoccupied with Chastity.

"Sure." I place my cell on the counter and sip the energy drink I opened an hour ago. It's flat, but still quenches my thirst.

"Your mother will be coming into town at the weekend. She has some business. It might be nice for us all to have dinner..."

Acid floods my muscles and liquefies my heart. "Does she want that?" I hear the need in my voice. It's not the tone of a grown man; it's the voice of a little boy who still needs his mother and misses her.

"Yes. It was her idea."

Her idea. She wants to go to dinner.

"Okay. Just let me know where and when."

"Great."

There's a spring in my step and it doesn't go unnoticed by Pride, who meets me at the coffee hut on campus.

"You got laid?" He slaps my back and offers a fist for me to bump.

"No, not yet." I shake my head, laughing, but it's strained. Was there a time limit on bedding Chastity?

"So, what's with the afterglow?" he snorts, sipping his coffee and wincing.

"Nothing, but while we're on the subject."

"The subject of nothing?" He smirks.

"You know what I mean. Is there a time limit?"

"Before we graduate would be good," he mocks me.

"So…no?"

"No, what?" Wrath asks, taking a seat with us. He's seemed off the last few days, worry clouding his eyes.

"Everything okay?" Pride asks, seeing the same strain.

"Yeah. I need to get to class." With that, he stands and saunters off.

"That was weird," I state.

"You're all weird," Pride grunts, tossing his full cup in the bin and swiping up his backpack.

"So…no?" I shout after him.

He ignores me. Asshole.

Lessons blend into one as the day ticks by slow as fuck.

Chastity: Carnival is in town.

Me: Carnival is always in town around you. You smell like cotton candy and apples.

Chastity: Is that a good thing?

Me: A very good thing. *Groans*

Chastity: If you take me, I'll let you kiss me in the tunnel of love.

Me: Deal.

TWENTY-FOUR

Anticipation tightens my muscles. My hands clench and unclench. Ever since she told me she would let me kiss her in the tunnel of love, I've had a one-track mind.

The outfit she opted to wear is driving me crazy. I'm about to bust a nut in my pants. The way she makes me feel is so unlike me, yet I don't want to pull away from it—I want to run toward it full force.

She holds back the pain, the sorrow and fear of not being good enough of surviving and my mother hating me for it. She makes the raging storm calm so I can breathe through it.

"You're staring again." She bites her lip, turning to face me.

"I'm not even going to deny it, you look incredible." I

tell her, raking my eyes down the summer dress that hugs her tits and waist, then flares out to flirt with the tops of her creamy thighs. She's sexy and innocence all wrapped up in a forbidden, delicious package.

"Let's get cotton candy." She beams, taking my hand and tugging me toward a stall.

"Two please," I say, but Chastity holds her finger up. "Just one. We'll share."

The girl manning the machine looks to me for confirmation.

"One."

Warm bodies move around us like movie extras. Tonight is just about the two of us. No one else exists in our reality.

Curling cotton candy around her finger, she makes a show of swiping her tongue out to gobble it up.

"You want a taste?" She smirks, pushing the pink cloud toward my face.

Yes I do.

Tugging her wrist, I catapult her toward me, then steal her squeal with my lips. I suck her fat bottom lip into my mouth and release it with a pop.

"Delicious." I wink. She just stares at me, breathing heavy and unrestrained.

"Kiss me, Rhett Masters," she demands, dropping the sticky sugar to the floor and throwing her arms around my neck.

Her supple body pushes hard against mine. "Kiss me like no one is watching," she breathes, her eyes shimmering with need.

Crashing my lips to hers, I drain the air from her lungs

and make my own seize.

My arms wrap around her torso, pinning her body to mine and I devour her, unrelenting. I roam her mouth with my tongue, exploring, caressing. Her body is so responsive to mine, she shudders in my arms, giving back everything I'm giving her.

Nerves and excitement spark in my gut like it's my first time. I can't explain it. All I know is this is new, this is real, this means something—like the world stopped and all there is is me and her.

Catcalls break through the heady haze of lust, and the world floods back in. I reluctantly slip her down my body and steady her when she sways.

"Get a room," someone snorts as they walk past, giving us stink eye.

Ignoring the audience, she pats her hand over her chest above her heart and smiles.

"I'm definitely living the best life. Wow." She giggles.

Grasping her behind her neck, I pull her head against my chest and kiss the top of her head, taking a moment to inhale the apple of her shampoo.

Her hands tighten in my shirt, and my cock strains and pulses against the zipper of my jeans, desperate to plunge into her heat.

Now that we've crossed the threshold of making out, she can't keep her lips from mine, and I can't keep my hands from roaming every curve of her taut body. Placing my palm against her lower back, I assist her very capable body into the seat of the love boat.

Who dreams this shit up? *Love boat?* And since when would I ever go on something like this?

Her smile brightens, and my heart stammers. *Since her, that's when.*

We've been on every ride there is, all but the house of mirrors. Bugs have bitten our flesh, and we're drunk on junk food and sugar candy. Chastity has been carrying around a giant pink bear I won on ring toss, refusing to let me dump him on a park bench.

She holds up our tickets for the mirror house and squeezes the fluffy bear through the guardrail.

Once inside, she teases me by attempting to hide. It's comical when she's carrying a bear bigger than her.

"I see you," I warn, jolting forward and reaching out. To my utter surprise, I hit glass and I stumble forward, knocking the mirror. It opens up like a secret door.

Shit.

"I totally got you," Chastity says from behind me.

"I think I broke the house."

Her mouth drops open, then closes. Intrigue glistens in her curious eyes. Stepping around me, she pokes her head through and slips inside.

"Where are you going?" I whisper-yell, following her ass inside, then pushing the mirror closed so no one sees what we've done.

It leads to a backstage type area where staff move around and set up. It's dark, and no one is here except us.

Her bear forgotten, she climbs me like I'm a tree, and I chuckle at her desperation. She's nothing like I thought she was going to be.

The heat of her pussy rests against my waist when she tightens her arms around my neck and legs around my torso.

Her lips attack me, kissing my mouth, my cheek, my neck. Gripping her ass, I growl and demand her mouth, conquering her quivering lips with my own. I find the back wall and push her against it so I can grind my cock against her heat. "Touch me, Rhett. Make the ache go away," she pleads between kisses.

Her hips wiggle, needy and persistent. There's no way I'm going to fuck her in the back hole of a carnival ride, but I can ease her tension. "Put your legs down," I command between nipping her lips and nibbling her neck.

Excruciatingly slow, she slides down my body, her pussy grazing the tip of my dick.

Cupping her cheeks, I pepper kisses over her face and lips, down her neck, across her chest. I skate my palms down the same path, unbuttoning the first couple of clasps on her dress, exposing the heaving mounds of her tits.

Allowing myself my small pleasures, I sink my teeth into her flesh, then lick away the sting when she moans out. "I'm going to take care of you," I comfort.

Her body is trembling so bad, she's almost lifting from the floor.

Skimming my hands down farther, I trace their path with my kisses over the fabric of her dress until I'm on my knees before her, the palms of my hand resting just below the hem of her dress.

"You sure you want this?" I ask, but she's answering, "Yes, yes," before I even finish the sentence.

Slipping my hands up her dress, I caress and tease her thighs, brushing the pad of my thumb over the cotton of her panties, when I reach my destination.

Moving to her hips, I tug down her panties, making her gasp.

When I get them to her ankles, she readily steps out, her chest heaving. She's already so fucking close to the edge.

Pulling her panties up to my face, I inhale her delicious, sweet essence. Pre-cum seeps from the tip of my dick, dampening my jeans.

Fuck. I've never been this horny from pleasuring a woman before, and I haven't even eaten her pussy yet.

Grasping her ankle, I lift it and place her foot on my shoulder.

She's mumbling curse words, which, from her mouth, is adorable. She knows what's coming.

Her in about one minute.

"Hold your dress up so I can look at your pretty pussy, Chastity."

"You are a bad boy," she whispers, and I bite down on my lip to stifle the chuckle her words bring. "Only when you need me to be," I inform her, leaning forward and licking her inner thigh.

Gathering up her dress, slow and deliberate, she exposes creamy flesh one inch at a time, until I'm looking at a small cluster of blonde curls sitting tidy on her mound, decorating the prettiest pussy I've ever seen. Her lips are smooth and thick like the lips of her mouth. Damn, she's perfection.

"I'm going to taste you now," I warn her.

Grasping her hip with one hand to steady her and wrapping the other arm around her ass, I crush her pussy to my face.

She jolts when my tongue parts her folds, tasting all that nectar hidden inside.

I fucking feast on her like a starving man getting to eat for the first time.

Her clit throbs against my tongue as I swirl and suck, adding pressure where she needs it, taking my cues from her moans and grip she has on my hair.

She moves her hips with me, taking what she needs, grinding and panting. "Oh god," she pleads, her legs shaking with impending release.

Slipping a hand from her hip, I suck a finger to lube it up, then reach between her legs, slipping the digit into her inviting center.

She clenches around it greedily as I plunge it deep, then pull it back, repeating the process. I speed up with her own breaths, until she's throbbing and pulsing around me, her release coating my hand.

Her body shudders, and she curls over me, gripping onto my hair tight.

Tight, warm, and fucking beautiful.

Once she gathers her bearings, I ease my finger out of her and look up into her flushed face as I slide it into my mouth, sucking every drop of her from it.

"Sweet like candy apples," I drawl, and she giggles, covering her mouth with her hand. Helping her get back into her panties, I take her hand and grab her bear, following the faint slither of light streaming in from the far end of the corridor type space.

There's an exit door that we push through to come out behind the stalls and rides.

"You ready to go?" I ask her, wrapping my arm around her waist.

She falls into me, melting into my side. "Yes. I'm spent."

Yeah she is.

TWENTY-FIVE

I couldn't bear to shower last night, to wash away Chastity's scent. She was everything and more—delicious, forbidden, sweet as sin.

Her body is so responsive, so needy, so perfect.

There were a lot of guys in high school who bitched about going down on a woman, but to me, there's nothing better—nothing more masculine than making a woman quiver and come on your tongue. I'd bathe in her juices if I could.

My thoughts wander to God. I have missed calls from him, but if I take the call, he'll ask me how I'm doing with my task, then he'll demand to know what's taking me so long and why I'm avoiding him.

I promised him, and made him promise me, we would do our tasks no matter what the consequences. But

I wasn't prepared to feel this way.

Slipping my phone into my pocket, I search the parking lot for one of his fancy ass cars, but like usual, he's absent from school, making avoiding him that much easier.

He isn't the only person I'm avoiding. Mrs. Griffin is also on my dodge list. Looking her in the eye and talking about things I don't want to share with her because I've found talking to Chastity oddly therapeutic isn't something I want to confess to her.

And knowing there's tension there between her and Chastity makes me not like her. Petty, but I chose a side the minute I sampled the lips of her stepdaughter.

My phone buzzes with a text from the woman in my every thought lately.

Chastity: Educated men are so impressive.

A smile chases up my cheek, and then I smell her before I have time to reply. Warm arms come around my midriff from behind. "Guess who?" she mumbles against my backpack.

"How many guesses do I get?" I tease, and she pinches my ass a little too roughly, making me jerk forward.

She rounds my body with a dreamy sparkle to her eyes.

"PDA in the corridor?"

Shrugging her petite shoulder, she closes in and whispers with a sultry drawl, "Corridors, carnival grounds."

My hand grasps out, capturing her behind her neck and tugging her to me, my lips taking hers in a deep kiss. Her small hand wraps around my wrist to hold herself steady as I steal the air from her lungs and flavor from her tongue.

She had strawberries for breakfast.

Forcing myself to release her, I relish the red bruising around her lips from my ministrations.

"Wow," she says in a wonderment filled breath. She's so adorable, it's painful.

"You not worried about people seeing you make out with the bad boy anymore?" I torment, but she doesn't bite. Instead, she stares at me like I made the sun rise.

"As long as he's only my bad boy, bring on the gossipers." Her tone is meek, searching for reassurance.

"If you're willing to be my good girl—only mine—then I promise to be a one-woman man." I grin to lighten the tension thickening around us. I've never had this kind of conversation before. I've always bailed before it ever got to this point. This is new ground for me, and there's these nervous, excited flutterings happening in my gut that make me happy and annoyed all at the same time. She's grinning so beautifully and big, her hope, her heart mine for the taking.

How could I let this happen? I'm fucking falling for this girl. This wasn't the plan. I have destructive secrets she can never find out about.

"Do you want to do something tonight?" she asks, checking her watch.

"I have dinner with my mother tonight, but I could see you after?"

Reaching onto her tiptoes, she drops a chaste kiss to my lips and backs away from me. "Call me."

Her body collides with another student, and she turns to splutter apologies, then sniggers back at me when the guy waves her off and doesn't stop.

She fades into the crowd, and I remember a line from her audio.

Me: Go wisely and slowly. Those who rush stumble and fall.

Send. It's perfect.

I hate that I'm sat making small talk with my dad and it's so fucking awkward and forced. Is it supposed to be this hard?

Dad's phone begins belting out some eighties song, causing the entire restaurant to turn their heads in our direction.

Answering the call, he gets to his feet, dropping his napkin on the empty plate. I'm starving and should be on the second course by now, but Mom is late.

I swirl the soda in the bottom of my glass. After sitting for forty minutes with my dad, I wish I'd added Jack Daniels to it.

A hand lands on my shoulder, jarring me and making me nearly knock the glass over.

My dad frowns, looking down at me. "Something happened with your mother's car. She's not going to make it."

My gut plummets. She's making excuses to bail on dinner. She's not ready to forgive me.

"We can still eat," my dad cuts in.

"No thanks. I said I'd meet some friends, so her not showing is better for me," I lie, brushing past him.

I need a drink.

Stumbling into the house, I almost fall through the threshold but catch myself.

"Are you drunk?" My dad grimaces.

"Nooope," I slur.

"Is that really your solution to something not going the way you wanted? Do you care what happened with your mother's car?"

"Noooope."

"You're being immature."

"Ha, says the man twucking a woman half his age."

Crossing his arms over his chest, he narrows his gaze on me. His arms look bigger, straining his shirt. He must be working out more. The brush with death scared him. I grin despite myself, and his stare gets even more squinty.

"You done?" I ask, trying not to sway on my feet.

"When you're done being a brat, you should give your best friend a talking to."

God? What the fuck does he have to do with anything? He's always had issue with God. Probably because he has more money than him.

I navigate the stairs and collapse into my room, missing the bed and landing with a thud on the floor. Motherfucker, that hurt, and it's uncomfortable as all hell down here, but I don't have the mobility skills to get up right now.

I'm on fire. Hell's fire scolds me, and hard droplets pelt down on me, attempting to put me out. But it's gasoline, not water.

My body rocks violently from the terror racing though me.

"Rhett, where are you?"

I hear Robbie's voice calling through the roaring of the fire.

The tree appears through the orange licks of flames and then I'm slipping through the mud beneath my feet. It's consuming me, hands pulling from beneath.

"No, stop, no," I choke out.

"Rhett?"

"I'm coming, Robbie," I cry, scraping at the mud, ignoring the pain all over me.

"Rhett. It's okay. It's okay." Robbie's voice morphs. "Wake up."

The rain turns cold—not acid rain, shower water.

Hard tiles against my skin. I'm panting heavily. Jerking awake, I try to stand, but slip back to my ass. I'm not being dragged into hell. I'm in my shower.

My eyes adjust, and Chastity fills my vision. She's soaked, fully dressed, sitting with me in the shower. What the hell's going on?

"Chastity?"

"Yes, oh god. Rhett, you scared me," she sobs, wrapping her arms around me.

"What are you doing here?" I croak, my throat stinging, a sour taste coating my tongue.

"You texted me to come over."

Had I?

"I found you facedown in your own vomit."

That would be the gross taste on my tongue then.

"I had to have your dad help me get you in the shower. He got upset and left."

"You mean mad?" I ask, a throb beginning in my skull.

Shivering, she stands to turn the blast of the shower off.

Her hair is stuck to her face, makeup streaks her eyes, and sorrow mars those precious features. "No, he wasn't mad, he was distressed when you were…" she pauses.

"Were what?"

"You were calling out for your brother and crying." She sniffs, taking my hand and interlocking our fingers.

Fuck. "I'm a mess."

"You're hurting, but it's okay. I'll face that pain with you. You're not alone, Rhett. You think I can't see the pain in your eyes, the sorrow soaking your body?" She grips my face, absorbing my agony with me.

"I won't pretend that I know how you feel, but if I could take some of that pain, that burden from you, I would, because I'm falling for you."

I drop my eyes from hers, too ashamed to look at her after allowing myself to get so reckless.

"Look at me. Look in my eyes. You're not alone anymore. It's you and me now, and I won't let you drown. You can't do this to yourself."

She holds me while I come apart. It's not a girl who's falling for a boy, or a boy tasked to seduce a girl he fell for. It's a human sharing another human's pain when they know they can't carry it on their own.

Getting dry and into dry clothes I admire Chastity wearing my tee, it drowns her but it's all kinds of sexy. I know in my heart that I want to see her wearing my shit after staying the night. After I've been inside her body. Made love to her in a way I've never adored a woman's body before.

"Do you want me to make you some coffee?" she asks brushing her hair back off her face with one of my mother's old brushes.

"No," I look her up and down. No way is my old man getting to see her in only a shirt.

"I'll get us some hot drinks, make yourself at home." I tell her noticing either her or my dad must have cleaned up the sick because the room smells of bleach and there's no puddle.

My feet are still unsteady as I take the stairs down to the kitchen, which is plunged into darkness.

Switching the light on, my heart leaps. My old man is sat nursing a mug of something sat at the breakfast bar.

"Why are you sitting in the dark?" My voice is hoarse, and my body feels like it's been through an intensive wash cycle.

"You have nightmares," he states.

I stop to watch him from the other side of the counter.

"I hear you at night. They stopped for a while, but tonight…" He frowns, running a hand through his hair, tugging on the strands.

"I drank too much," I confess.

"You blame yourself?"

He already knows the damn answer to that.

"We all blame me," I correct.

He swipes at his face. Is he crying?

"It's not your fault," he rasps.

Liar.

"Denial. It was just easier to place the blame elsewhere. Losing Robbie was the hardest thing I've ever had to face in my life." He admits.

He's never opened up like this before. I wish I would've heard it months ago.

"It was me." He croaks.

My hands grip the counter, my knuckles turning white.

"What was you?"

Sniffling, he wipes his forearm across his nose. "I told Robbie to walk." He breaks.

My head swims. I don't understand. "When…how?" I shake my head. He's making no sense.

"He wasn't feeling good. Called me using his friend's phone. I told him he had to wait for you, but when he said he felt queasy, I told him to walk down to my office."

He tugs at his hair, punishing himself.

Tension stiffens my body.

"Why? Why couldn't you get him?" I demand.

Sickness threatens to spill out of me from his confession.

He's known this shit all this time and kept it too himself. He's a selfish cunt. Poor Robbie, let down by us both.

My darkest day was losing Robbie, that darkness has been cloaking me ever since and he's had this information this the whole time.

He's staring at me now, chin quivering, water leaking from his eyes.

Fuck him.

"I was mid-fuck." He confesses. "Melissa was leaving for a vacation, and I wanted to get one last fuck in before I didn't see her for two weeks."

The utensil holder in front of me flies across the room before I even register throwing it at him.

"You make me sick," I growl.

My entire body threatens to collapse at the weight of his words.

It was his fault—not mine. I didn't kill Robbie.

"And what if he made it to the office?"

"We were finishing up," he confesses, disgust on his own tongue.

My mind replays that night over and over, the time it would take to walk twenty minutes maybe? Thirty for Robbie whose legs were shorter than mine.

"Did you wonder why he didn't show up?" I seethe.

Gulping he takes back his seat and swigs whatever's in his mug.

"Your mother." He exhales before continuing, "She caught us." He grumbles into his cup.

That night is the night she caught him fucking his secretary?

"That's why she wanted you to pick Robbie up, she was casing my fucking office building like a PI."

Rounding the counter with revived energy I push him hard making him stumble from the stool and stumble back across the kitchen.

Pointing a damning finger at him I growl. "Don't fucking blame her or make a mockery of what she had to do to prove her own sanity wasn't playing tricks on her. Everyone knew you were a piece of shit but not her, she always had your back. And you blew it. For that blonde piece of ass? Really, is she worth it?"

Turning on my heel, I can't even look at him. Urges to pound the shit out of him until he's pulp of blood and bone pull at my restraint, but he's fucked my life up enough, he gets no more of it.

Walking into my room I feel like a different person. A burden heavy on my soul has lifted. "You ok?" Chastity asks from her perched position on my bed.

"Yeah, I think I am."

Her lips turn up into a smile and she pats the space next to her.

"Can you stay the night?" I ask.

She bites her lip nervously, a blush coloring her cheeks. "Just sleep, Chas, please?"

"Ok. I'll call my dad and tell him I'm crashing at Maggie's." She attempts to get up, but I hold my hand up to stop her.

"You stay and call him, I need to make a call of my own, I'll go outside."

All my demons race around inside my head as I wait for Pride to arrive. I text him as soon as I left my old man to weep in the misery he created. This couldn't be done over the phone.

Ten minutes later he's pulling up across the street. There's a nervous energy pulsing through me with what I'm about to do, but I know it has to be done. There's no other way.

"You look like shit," he says, meeting me halfway down the path.

"Good to see you too, asshole."

He nods his head at Chastity's car and smirks.

"That the reason I'm here? You got something for me?"

Shoving my hand in my pocket, I close my eyes briefly before pulling out the coin.

"I do, but not what you think." I place the gold metal into his palm and wait for the lecture that doesn't come.

"It is what I expected. The tasks are not made for all of us, and to be honest, I'm not keen on a lot of this shit. Just know you can't control or forfeit what comes next. If you do..."

"I'm out. I know."

I just can't lose anything else. As if reading my thoughts Pride places a hand on my shoulder. "Losing a sibling is fucking soul crushing, believe me I know, so if she helps you, even forget for a second then, I wouldn't risk it all for a task either."

Fuck. I exhale a heavy breath. I needed to hear that so badly.

TWENTY-SIX

Every night this week Chastity's come over to sleep. She's been creeping out down the stupid lattice fence on the side of her house and meeting me at the bottom of her street to be whisked away to my lair.

She's eager to try new things, her hands exploring new areas each night, but I'm terrified of disappointing her, ruining her confidence when I'm unable to come.

Since my dad's confession I haven't been having nightmares, but that could also be due to the fact Chastity has been sharing my bed every night.

Leaving the bathroom, I flick the switch and almost fucking come in my pants.

Chastity stands at the foot of my bed waiting for me but she's not wearing her usual tee that she borrows from my stack. She's wearing nothing at all.

I can't take her all in fast enough, my eyes computing and storing every inch of creamy flesh, her hard, rosy-tipped nipples, the channel of her naval leading to the neat little cluster of blonde curls.

My mouth waters and I think about licking her pussy until she's delirious and can't even function.

She moves toward me, her movements slow and suggestive, but her hands flexing gives away her anxiety of this moment.

Unsure fingers reach for my waistline tugging on the hem of my boxers. Clasping my hand over hers I whisper a strained. "Don't"

My cock swells with need tenting the fabric but I'm fucking terrified. Who the hell am I?

"It's ok, I want this." She pleads.

My face contorts into frustration and pain. "Since Robbie, I struggle, I can't..."

"Shhh," she calms, placing a hand over my heart.

"It's just us here,"

She taps in rhythm of our in-sync, erratic heartbeats.

Da-dum. Da-dum. Da-dum. Da-dum. Da-dum.

"Step out of the nightmares, silence the voices that tell you you're not worthy of this." She begs imploring me with her hypnotic gaze.

"You didn't kill your brother. It was a shitty accident, unfair and cruel but he wouldn't want you to self-blame, to stop yourself from living, to stop yourself from feeling, from having someone who loves you."

Da dum, da, dum, da dum, da dum, da dum.

"Your head's a storm, turbulent and destructive. You need to find the center, the calm. Let me be that for you."

Taking my hand, she leads me to the bed and sits on

the edge looking up at me through her thick lashes.

"Tell me how you release, how you touch yourself." She pleads slipping my boxers down my ass, my throbbing cock springing free like a fucking jack in the box. Boo baby. Her eyes expand, and she swipes her tongue out to dampen her bottom lip. Fuck me.

"Show me how you do it to yourself Rhett."

Fuck she's everything a guy dreams about in a tight little package. I'd never have believed she was this sensual little spitfire if I wasn't seeing it for myself. I've hit the girlfriend lottery.

Shit, *girlfriend*. I have a girlfriend.

"Rhett, do you need something to think about?" She bites her lip and then blows my fucking mind. Leaning back on her elbows she brings her feet up to rest on the edge of the mattress. Her sexy folds opening up to display all that pretty pink pussy.

Sucking two fingertips into her mouth she makes a scene swirling her tongue around them and then she pulls them free and lowers them to her pussy, massaging her clit just for me.

Clear pre-cum seeps over the tip of my hard, throbbing dick. I ache to mount her like a caveman and rut on her until I spurt my seed into her.

Gripping my dick, I stroke, and this makes her breathing hitch. Her tits heave with her uneven exhales. She keeps the pace I set, stroking for her.

Every tug feels almost painfu,l the veins bulging with the strain of being so god damnhard for her.

Her pussy clenches, juices glistening in her tight, little hole.

"Come for me, Rhett. Come on me, baby." She begs,

her moans reaching fever pitch. Her back arches and her words are the sexiest thing I've ever heard. Heat rips up my spine, muscles pull tight and euphoric waves crash over me as I move between her legs and the ribbons of come paint her flesh.

Ripples of shuddering pleasure pouring out of me, warm liquid need covering her torso and nipples, dripping down on her pussy.

If I could replicate this into art form I would hang it on my wall forever.

"Fuck." I groan out. My legs shaking with the intense release. My cock thickens again immediately and I'm not waiting to feel her. Leaning over I kiss her lips.

"Thank you." I tell her before devouring her mouth. Lifting her under the armpits I scoot her up the bed, her hands tug at my hair frantic as our lips dance and tongues duel.

Her tits press into my chest as I bring our bodies skin on skin, her thighs wrap around my waist. She's fucking hungry and I plan to feed her all she can handle.

My fluids coat our flesh as I grind my hard on into the crease of her folds.

"Don't tease me." She pleads.

"I don't want to rush and hurt you." I tell her honestly.

"I'm not a virgin, Rhett." She suddenly tenses.

Well damn.

"High school boyfriend of three years. I finally gave in and let him take my virginity. He pressured, then told everyone, and it got back to my father. He threatened to send me to boarding school."

I fucking hate this prick. As soon as I'm not on the edge of entering her body, I'm going to ask for this motherfucker's name and pay him a visit.

"I'm sorry…did you think…?" She softens under my body.

"No. I wish your first time was better for you, but it doesn't change anything for me."

Why should it, I've fucked more women than had hot dinners.

"It's my second time, but my first time with someone I love." She whispers.

"Me too," I tell her honestly. A contented sigh leaves her body and then we're touching, feeling, loving each other.

When I finally push into the warmth of her body, I know I'm home. She's my new home. My everything.

TWENTY-SEVEN

Getting up at the crack of dawn so Chastity can sneak back into her house before her dad wakes is comical. I've been sleeping like a fucking baby since she's been tiring me out all week. She's insatiable. I watch her ass wiggle as she climbs the lattice to her roof.

Last weekend while her dad and Lillian were out of town for a conference I came by and reinforced the thing to make sure it was safe and sturdy for her. They'll never notice because it's down the side of the house that's covered mostly by shrubs.

She crawls through the window and blows me a kiss, when I make it back to my car I already have a text from her.

Chastity: Parting is such sweet sorrow

Before I reply, my phone beeps again with an

incoming message from Pride.

Pride: Can you meet me before class?

Me: sure, where?

Pride: initiation place.

Nerves are back eating away my insides, a yawn rips from me as I step from foot to foot to ward off the morning cold.

The place is fucking freezing, the stone holding in the cold and cocooning you like a tomb. Footfalls sound and Pride pushes into the chapel room. "Hey man."

My fingers are almost numb when I reach out for the card he offers. No small talk. It must be fucking bad.

"You've got to be kidding," I snort reading the only line that matters out loud.

"Seduce the dean's wife?"

It's not his fault, but my fury is aimed at him right now.

"I don't have any part in the tasks," he informs me, straightening his shoulders. "I fucking hate this as much as you do. I just want it to be over."

Snatching the card from me, he lights it on fire and drops it to the floor.

"I can't fucking do this!" I breathe, dropping on my haunches and holding my head in my hands. After dad's confession, I want out from him more than before, but at this price?

This would kill Chastity, and would Lillian even be seducible?

Of course she is. I haven't met a woman who isn't.

"Just make it quick. In and out," Pride grunts.

"It's not a drop by to say hi, they want me to fuck her," I grate out.

Shuffling his feet, he sighs loud enough for it to reach my ears.

"The Elite comes as a price, as with everything in life. Sacrifices have to be made"

Don't I fucking know it.

Sitting in the car staring at the stone building already late for my first class, I will my legs to move but I'm frozen. The bottle of Jack Daniels sits on the passenger seat willing to offer me courage.

Drink up let the alcohol convince me I'm still this guy. My stomach rolls and I grab the bottle and toss it in the backseat.

I can't fuck her, no way.

There's nothing that will convince me I'm the same guy I was before Chastity, and she deserves more than this.

More than that.

I know she only has two classes this morning and then she's done for the day, so I whip out my phone and text her to meet me at my house for lunch.

By lunch, I mean feasting on each other.

She bounds up the drive to meet me where I'm sat on the steps like a love-sick pre-teen waiting for a love note to be delivered.

I feel relieved.

"Hey, lover" she beams, launching herself at me as I get to my feet. Her arms wrapping around my neck, legs around my waist.

"You hungry?" I growl.

"Yep." She grins.

"For food or cock?" I tease. Her cheeks turn rosy pink and she burrows her head into my neck giggling.

I've fucked her five ways from Sunday in multiple positions. Had my cock, fingers and tongue inside her pussy, yet she still blushes at the crude words. She's adorable. Then I hear it, it's faint but clear enough. "Cock."

Fuck yeah.

TWENTY-EIGHT

The knock at the door brings a chuckle to my lips. She must have forgotten something. She's a fool for coming back for it because now I'm going to keep her here longer.

Her face isn't the one that greets me at my bedroom door. Mrs. Griffin's is.

It's like the fates realign to make my tasks easy for me, but it's more tormenting than anything.

"What are you doing here?"

She pushes into my room, placing her handbag on my desk.

"Nice place," she compliments.

"Thanks? How did you get in here?"

"You've been avoiding me. The terms of your enrollment were made clear to you."

Fuck.

"I think I know why you've been avoiding me."

The steam from the shower begins billowing from the open door. Holding up a finger, I excuse myself to turn the water off. Are guidance counselors allowed to make house calls to student's bedrooms?

Turning the shower off, the vent kicks in, clearing the steam, and my eyes bug out of my head when I turn to find Mrs. Griffin in the doorway wearing nothing but black lace lingerie and black stockings.

What the fuck is happening?

"I see the way you look at me, the way you check out my pictures, and it's okay. I feel it too. How can we deny something that feels so powerful?" she says, sauntering her half-naked ass over to me.

Her arms come up around my neck, and cement fills my bones.

Did I fall asleep? How the hell could she think I looked at her some way—and act on it?

Not that I did...have...do—fuck, now my internal voice sounds like Chastity. *Shit...Chastity.*

I grab her arms and pull them from around my neck, placing them against her chest. "Nope," I state, matter-of-fact.

"What?"

"Hard pass. Not happening. Not interested."

"But..."

Damn woman. She's clearly never been turned down before. Truth is, before Chastity, I may have fucked her for shits and giggles, but after Chastity? No way in hell. I don't want to fuck another soul.

Lillian's lips pull into a thin line, her eyes narrowing.

"You don't want this?"

It's then I see it. My stomach rolls and, heat explodes up my spine. Under the blacklight God had fitted in here, The Elite mark glows.

"You're Elite?" I shake my head, grabbing her wrist and straightening her arm. She attempts to tug it free from my grasp, but she's weaker than piss.

I lift her arm above her head. Tucked right near her armpit is The Elite mark, Envy written beneath their logo.

She's Envy for the class of god knows when.

Why would they want me to fuck a member?

I weaken my hold, and she snatches back her arm. "You'll regret this," she snaps.

I follow her retreat into my room. She bends to swipe up her jacket, the only thing covering her scantily clad form.

"Did The Elite put you up to seducing me?" I ask, bewildered.

She rounds on me with pity in her features, shaking her head at me.

"Why would The Elite want me to seduce you?" she snaps. Good question. It's just fucking weird I'm given the task to fuck her and here she is doing the job for me.

"I thought you wanted this." She laughs without humor, slipping her shoes on and grabbing her purse.

"I'll see you for our session next week," she throws over her shoulder, slamming my bedroom door like nothing happened.

Fuck this, I need to talk to Pride.

I get to the bottom of my street and frown when I see God's car parked on the corner with him inside. Pulling up next to him, I lower my window, and he does the same.

"Hey," he says, hesitant.

"What are you doing here?"

"You said do whatever it takes," he reminds me.

"Yeah well, I guess some of us are willing to go the extra mile. My mom's fucking car, God? After everything she went through with Robbie?"

Grinding his jaw he smacks his hand on the steering wheel.

"It's just a car, she now has a new one. I'm only in The Elite for you!" He punctures the word *you* with a growl.

"And now I hear you handed in your coin? From fucking Pride, of all people, I hear this?"

What's his problem with Pride?

"I'm out of the Elite," I state, and sickness at the thought of actually being out stirs in my gut. I don't know what I plan to do about tuition and living and anything else right now. I can't see past Chastity.

She's all that matters. I know he won't understand that, not until it happens to him one day.

It's like being held underwater your entire life, and then finally being pulled up and taking a breath.

"You needed The Elite. This was all your idea—your plan," he fumes.

I nod my head, agreeing. "I know, but they wanted something I couldn't give them. I'm going to tell Pride and the others at our next meeting. They'll replace me."

With that, he rolls his window up and screeches out of the estate.

TWENTY-NINE

Sacrifice. That's when you know you love someone, when you're willing to give up something you want for something you need. I need her, her happiness, her smiles, touch, love.

Handing my coin over was one of the hardest things I've done. But it was the only way. There was no way I could complete my task, and this new one would do damage to Chastity too, all to get at her dad? Why could it not be for me to just rough the fucker up?

It fucking sucks, but there's no other way.

Pride is standing in the parking lot when I arrive on campus, leaning against Greed's car, arms folded, a crease marring his forehead.

Pulling into the space next to him, he comes around and gets in my passenger side.

"Hey," I say, warily.

"I know it must have been hard for you to do it, but it's enough. You're in," he tells me, and I frown, confused.

He drops my coin in my palm and nods. "I've informed the other's of your status."

What the fuck is he talking about?

He takes my confusion with surprise. "The video?" He says, like I know what the hell he's talking about.

Getting out his phone, he plays with the screen, and then my cell beeps.

My insides coil and the blood drains from my veins.

It's a video of Chastity and me at the carnival in the back of the magic mirror, or whatever the fuck it's called.

Me eating her pussy. Rapture caught on her expression as I bring her to climax. Motherfucker.

The film is on a cell phone being held from what looks like just outside the back exit door.

Shame and guilt saturate me. This will kill Chastity.

"You didn't send me that?" Pride asks.

"What? Fuck no. Where did it come from?"

"No number. I thought you must have sent it from the phone it was caught on. So you didn't know you were being filmed?"

Is he fucking dumb? "No," I grate out, my anger flaring.

"Well…shit."

"Have you shown that to anyone?" Oh god, what if it's gone viral by someone out to get me, or her, or us both, or just someone caught us and is being a dick.

"I handed it over to The Elite, Rhett. I'm sorry, brother. I thought you had a change of heart."

"Fuck. Fuck. Fuck," I roar, slamming my hands

against the steering wheel.

"Maybe there's a way we can track the sender?" he grunts.

"It doesn't fucking matter now. It's out there." I exhale, closing my eyes to ward off the impending headache.

"I'm sorry, Rhett."

With that, he opens the door and slams it shut on his departure.

Walking through the corridors is a special kind of torture. I see everyone. Usually I'm lost in my own thoughts, but not today. I'm studying every damn person I pass.

Do they know? Have they seen it? Was it them?

Avoiding Chastity is its own form of torment. She's the one I want to be with in a crisis. I'll lose her over this. Will she know it wasn't me? Surely the camera angle proves it.

I drag my feet for the weekly appointment with Lillian. Things are just too fucking weird for her to demand I still come to see her. I'm going to tell her today. It ends. Ask her what she knows about The Elite.

Raised voices sound from her door, garnishing worried looks from a girl in the waiting area.

It's Chastity's voice. *No.*

Pushing the handle, I open the door and my world tilts, my heart imploding. Red blotchy eyes, tear-soaked cheeks, a phone playing the video in her hand. Her cunt stepmother leans against her desk in front of her, arms folded, a smirk on her lips.

"Chas," I croak.

Her chest rises and falls with her heartbreak.

Getting to her feet, she hands the phone back to Lillian and barges past me.

It's over. I know it without her telling me, and the loss hits me like a tidal wave, knocking me off kilter.

Slamming the door closed, rage races through my blood like a drug.

"You fucking bitch," I growl.

With a non-committal shoulder shrug, the whore smirks. "She had to know who she was getting involved with."

"Like you give a fuck about her," I snort.

"She's my stepdaughter. Of course I do. She my husband's pride and joy," she sneers the last sentence, hate clear in her delivery.

"No one can compare to his sweet Chastity, even though he tries to find girls who do." She spits her venom—jealously, hate, vengeance.

"Preserving her innocence is his concern, so it's also mine."

"You'll regret this," I warn, throwing her own threat back at her. Her cold, beady eyes narrow, and she laughs.

"This meeting is over." She points to the door. "Close the door on the way out."

"Fuck you, cunt," I bark, slinging open her door. I waltz through it, letting it slam against the hinges and bounce back open.

Breaking into a jog, I check the girls' bathroom and every corner Chastity could have fled to, but come up empty. Pushing out one of the exits, I race down the steps and come up short when Maggie stands in my path.

"Where is she?" is all I say. I don't need a lecture from her.

"I was going to ask you. She took off like a bat out of hell. She was…" She inhales and exhales. "I've never seen her so upset. Broken."

I broke her.

Getting in my car, I drive to her house and breathe out when I see her car parked badly in her driveway. At least she came home and got here safe.

Banging on the door gets me no answer, so I try the handle, but it's locked.

Fuck.

"Chastity," I call up to her window, desperation bleeding into my voice.

Silence.

After four more attempts, she appears in her window, the glass raised up so she can lean out.

"Why are you here?" She sounds so hoarse, so lost, so defeated. I did this to her, made her feel this pain.

"I love you," I say. Truth is all I have.

"I was a task to you. A dare!" she screams.

"That's not true," I plead.

"You let someone film us and then shared it. With her, Rhett. Of all people," she sobs.

"It wasn't me. I didn't…I would never…"

"Stop lying. You've been caught. The game is over. You won."

"It's not a fucking game. Please don't do this. I need you."

She studies me in silence for a few minutes, then shakes her head. Her eyes dart to something behind me, a passerby stopping with her dog to be a nosey cunt.

"Fuck off, you nosey bitch," I bark, trying to find any place for my anger. Her jaw unhinges, and she scuttles off, pulling the poor dog along with her.

"You're a real piece of shit, you know that, right?"

"Chas, let me in. Let's talk about this please."

"There's nothing you can say that will make this okay. You let me love you." She chokes on the words, her hand coming to her mouth like she's going to vomit.

"Don't ever call me. When you see me in the corridor, pretend I don't exist—because I don't for you anymore."

A knife would have been less painful. Defeat wraps me in a chokehold, and I struggle to fill my lungs with needed air. It's over.

Love is more dangerous than lust. I knew it and played into the game unwillingly, until it was too late. I lost.

Dragging my ass back to the car, I grab the bottle from the backseat and drown in self-pity.

The price of loving someone is too much, too hard. I'm not going to make it through this.

Liquor warms my blood and gives me false hope, then dooming misery, when I try over and over for her to come to the door. Hours pass as I go between her house and the car.

My motor functions become less coordinated. She doesn't even come to the window, and when I tried to climb the flower wall thingy, I fell in the bush—and I'm pretty sure cat shit.

My feet stumble as I throw my hands in the air, defeated. It's really over. Tears burn my eyes, and I don't care if I'm being a pussy. This shit hurts more than I ever thought possible.

Dousing my throat with the Jack Daniels, I find

myself walking past the car and down the road, through the brush, until I find the hidden park.

I pull my cell phone out and drop it. Every time I try to pick it up, I stumble a little. It's the worst game ever. Finally grasping it, I open it on God's name and dial the number.

Two rings and he answers. It doesn't matter what's happened with us he will always be my brother.

"I'm in," I slur.

"Rhett?"

"I'm in and I lost her." I hiccup, then croak, "It cost me her. Someone recorded us. She saw it. Thinks it was me." I'm crying, the words slurred and my heavy breathing making a weird sound into the phone.

"Where are you?"

"Nowhere. I'm lost at sea again. She was my lighthouse, my Juliet, my good girl."

"Rhett, where the fuck are you?"

I end the call and go lay on the slide. It's cold and damp, but I'm too drunk to give a shit.

The stars spin above me. When did the sun set?

Voices echo through the trees, and I must be dreaming because it sounds like God.

"There," someone shouts. Is that Sloth?

I try to sit up and focus, but my eyesight blurs.

"Woah, this is cool," Sloth says.

"It's creepy," God tells him.

"Rhett?"

"How did you find me?" I wheeze, my throat raw.

"Tracked your cell phone. You have GPS on."

Well…shit.

"You should turn that off. Anyone can trace it."

"It's probably how someone caught him and the girl…"

Fuck.

"Thanks for coming for me, God, I know things are weird between us right now." I hiccup.

Shaking his head he makes a pstt sound.

"Dude, I'm pissed I had to come traipsing through mud and forest and shit to save your drunken ass."

"I'm dying," I confess, scrubbing my hands over my face. I want to be left here to rot.

Let the land claim me back.

Gripping my arm, God tugs me up, slings my arm over his shoulder, and grips around my waist. "Not today you're not," he grumbles.

I can't walk. My body feels too heavy and night keeps threatening to steal me away.

"I'm surprised he's still breathing. He smells like a brewery."

"Gone," I mumble. "She's gone, lost her."

"Shhh. Like always, I'll figure this shit out," God tells me.

THIRTY

Toy soldiers dance over my scalp, banging their drums. Woozy sickness stirs in my gut, and thirst grips me. I crack an eye open and sigh when I see water on my bedside table.

I briefly remember God tossing me on the bed last night. How the fuck I ended up with him is a mystery.

And then the pain crashes into me, stealing my breath.

Chastity. As if my heart beckoned her, she appears in my line of vision. Am I dreaming?

"Am I dreaming?" I ask, rubbing my eyes.

"God came to me last night. He confessed it was him who filmed us and you didn't know. Some task that was too important to fuck up or something that made no sense to me." She shakes her head. "Point is, I know you didn't film me…us…it…"

"I would never. I'm so sorry this happened."

Nodding her head, she frowns. "I know you are. I don't understand all this. Tasks...and was I a dare or something?"

Sitting up despite my skull cracking into two, I reach for her and almost cry like a bitch when she doesn't pull away. Her little body lowers to the bed, and she studies my hands holding hers.

"Have you ever heard of The Elite?" I ask, laying it all out there.

Her eyes snap up to mine, then she closes them.

"Of course you're part of The Elite." She exhales a shuddering breath.

So she has heard of it.

"My father spoke about The Elite to me. I was to tell him If they ever approached me."

"Have they?"

"No." She shakes her head.

"When you're recruited by them, you're given a task to complete."

"Okay."

"I met you before I was ever given my task. It was pure coincidence the two mixed."

I'm not explaining this well.

"Getting into The Elite meant everything to me, Chas. It was all I wanted—until you. I gave my chance up because I refused to hurt you like that."

"I don't understand why they would want you to hurt me?"

"Me either. I'm sorry. But you should know, Lillian is a member, Chas, she wears their mark."

Sighing heavy she shakes her head. "That doesn't

surprise me even though it should. Her family, her brother, is a very powerful man."

Gripping her hands tighter I implore.

"I didn't know initiation would be something so …"

"Disgusting? Degrading? Personal? Illegal?" She says, pulling her hands free from my hold.

No. She can't leave me.

"Please don't leave me." I put my vulnerability out there. Raw and true.

"Your best friend's an asshole and I'm not okay with what he did or you being a part of this Elite. They're bad news, Rhett. But those few hours without there being an us was like death. Never again. Let's make a pact now that nothing will come between us again."

"I promise."

My world centers when she crawls into my lap and allows me to hold her.

I inhale her scent, touching every inch of her. I'm never letting go.

I know God wasn't the one who filmed us. He wouldn't stoop to that shit. He only told her that to bring her back to me.

And I'm never letting her go.

THIRTY-ONE

"You need to forgive him." I tell my mom as she picks at her food, sat opposite me in the restaurant. We're finally having our dinner together, minus my father.

"He trashed my car, Rhett. I've known that boy his whole life, love him like my own."

I stop eating and implore her. "I know and that's why you need to offer him a little slack, he would never intentionally do anything to hurt you."

Holding up her hand she nods. "I know that, and of course his father can be persuasive into letting things go." She rolls her eyes.

"Four even offered to pay off your school fees." She snorts offended.

"Like I need him to put my son through school."

"Not when I have my own father to make me earn the tuition fees." I mock.

"I pay your fees and all I expect is effort with classes, Rhett, that's not too much to ask." She scoffs sipping her drink.

Wait, wait… "What?" I ask, bewildered.

My mother sits opposite me, looking a little confused.

"I paid your school fees at the start of term. Why would you think your father was paying?"

Motherfucker.

She doesn't give me time to answer before she speaks again.

"I've also invested in a property I want you to consider moving into. I'll stay there too, if you'll have me?"

Is she for real?

"I've missed you, Mom."

Tears fill her eyes.

"I've missed you too, so much. I know you thought I was being harsh on you leaving like I did, and I don't blame you for not wanting to see me, but—"

"Wait," I blurt, cutting her off.

"You thought I didn't want to see you?"

She plays with her napkin, tearing it into tiny pieces. "Your father said you were angry that I left."

"That piece of shit," I growl. "He told me you weren't ready to see me!"

My mother turns white as a sheet. "You're my son. I wouldn't never not want to see you."

Reaching across the table, she grabs my hand. "I love you, Rhett. More than anything in this world."

Emotion clogs my throat. I didn't know how bad I needed to hear that from her until she said it. My own tears build in my eyes, and I squeeze them closed to will away the salty drops.

"You wouldn't believe what I went through to try to get out of Dad paying for my school." I chuckle, but it's strained.

Her body stiffens, and she takes a sip of her wine.

"I do, actually. Your father informed me about The Elite. I'm not going to lie, Rhett, it breaks my heart you're involved with them."

That makes me sit back in my chair.

"You know about The Elite?"

Laughing nervously, she holds up her hand to flag down the waiter.

"The Elite have been around long before you were even a dream of mine." She smiles over at me. The waiter fills her glass, and she thanks him before continuing.

"They've always wanted to recruit one of us. Our family owns businesses in this town. They've wanted to relieve us of them since your grandfather owned them."

Old memories must flit in her mind because a reminiscent smile touches her lips.

"I was offered a place in The Elite, them knowing I'd inherit my father's legacy."

She snorts, then takes another sip of her wine, swirling the red liquid around her glass.

"I wasn't interested. My father had informed me all I needed to know about them then. They're bad news. You will always be in their grasp and god forbid their debt, Rhett."

She exhales before continuing.

"Paying for your school fees, and with everything that happened with Robbie, I thought they wouldn't attempt…" She sighs. "Just be careful, Rhett. You're all I have left in this world."

I wish we had this conversation months ago.

"I thought they could help me with me going into law. I want to go into law so asshole drunk drivers don't get off with fines when they kill kids," I growl.

Sighing, she shakes her head, closing her eyes briefly.

"Rhett, he got off because of The Elite. He's Elite."

Thud. Thud. Thud.

Jumping from my seat, I race to the toilet and vomit.

This whole damn time. Those motherfuckers. That's the service you get with The Elite. They get you a fine when you kill a kid. What have I done?

Swilling my mouth with water, I spit and compose myself. I'm sick of drama in my life, the happy always being over shadowed by darkness. I need to live in the sunshine for a while. Flourish instead of wilting.

Getting back to the table, I collapse into my seat.

"You okay?" my mother asks.

"I have someone in my life," I say, squirming a little. "Someone I want you to meet," I add.

She beams at me, her smile reaching her eyes and becoming infectious. Before she can control herself, she squeals a little and claps her hands. "Rhett, oh god, that makes me so happy."

"Me too, Mom."

THIRTY-TWO

Pushing into Lillian's office she doesn't even get to her feet when I storm in like a hurricane landing on shore.

I slap the paper I had mom write out for me onto her table and gesture to her pen.

"Sign this."

Squinting her eyes at me she picks the paper up.

"What is it?"

"It's a letter signing me off from your services. No more meetings. Ever."

I grate out.

"And I should sign this because?"

"Because if you don't I'm going to fucking ruin you, or kill you, I've not decided yet."

She cackles like a fucking witch.

"Amusing as your threats are, I have no reason for

you to continue our sessions. There's nothing I can do for someone with your issues." She snorts picking up the pen and scribbling her signature on the dotted line.

"Close the door on your way out." She seethes handing me the paper.

Snatching it from her hand I waltz out leaving the door open.

After filing the letter with the office so it's on my file, I exit the college and breathe in the fresh air. I'm about to head for the car lot when I see Sloth coming towards me. I've never known anyone as laid back as him, even his movements are slow like he has all the time in the world.

"Hey." I reach my fist out and he bumps it with his own.

"What's up, man?" I encourage him into conversation.

"I've actually been looking for you, God said you were on campus."

"You found me." I grin, shoving my bag up my shoulder and starting a slow walk. He falls in line, his heavy boots scraping the concrete as he does.

"I have something for you." He hands me a brown, large envelope.

Intrigued I stop to open it, pulling out a picture.

"His father owns nightclubs, he's the youngest of six brother's and has bouts of depression. It started when he found out he'd raised two sons then found out they weren't his, his wife had been having a nine year affair with his oldest brother."

I don't need to hear all this. It doesn't matter.

"One day he came home to an empty house. She left him and was divorcing him so she could marry his brother. To make matters worse the family sided with the eldest and expected him to just accept this."

It's no excuse. I don't fucking care.

"He became dependent on alcohol to ease the pain of it all." He says through a cloud of smoke.

Is that fucking weed on campus? God's rubbing off on him. They think the rules don't' apply to them.

"One evening he's drinking shots feeling sorry for himself when he gets a call from one of the kids he raised, they want to come home."

I. DON'T. CARE.

"The only thing on his mind is his kid needs him."

More puffs.

"He gets in his truck and the weather turns nasty, he drank too much, he shouldn't be driving but.."

"But he fucking chose to get in that truck knowing he was over the limit." I bark. "How the hell do you even know this shit, where did you get his name and picture?" I query.

Shrugging his shoulders he flicks his lighter open and shut. "He goes to my father's church, I like to get baked and sit in the confessional booth."

Frowning at him I shake my head. "He can never repent for this. Nothing will ever be enough."

"I know, and so did he, they found him dead this morning. He hung himself."

I blanche at his words. There's no relief or pleasure filling the crater sized hole left by Robbie's death.

"He hated that his family ties got him off."

"The Elite got him off." I correct.

"The Elite aren't what you thought they were, Rhett."

"Yeah I'm working that out, the question is, if you already knew that then why did you want in?"

Smirking he backs away. "Who says I wanted in, maybe they *wanted* me in."

Well that's cryptic as fuck.

Nodding my head I fold my arms over my chest trying to feel anything about the mans death, but its weird. I hated him for what he took from us. I wished for his death a million times over, but this isn't how I wanted it to be. He was a victim himself. And he handed out his own justice, taking that from us too.

Tossing the photo in the trash I gulp down air to fill my lungs and leave the thoughts of the man there with it.

It's over. At least it's over.

I'm part of The Elite now, and I hate that they recruit people who are so willing to allow things like Robbie's death be swept under the rug.

And that they recruit vile women like Lillian into the fold. But maybe being part of the society doesn't have to be a bad thing. We can make changes from within. I know Rush has more to say on the matter and we'll get into it at some point, right now though I need to take the good and run with it. Give my mind some peace.

THIRTY-THREE

Throwing my keys on the table, I offer my old man a middle finger and take the last box out to the moving truck.

"Good riddance to that house of lies," I tell Chastity.

"You're not going to miss the place?"

Tapping my head, I grin. "I have all the memories I need up here. Everything else I need is coming with me."

Scooping her up, I carry her upfront and place her ass into the passenger seat, then push her cute ass over so I can climb in next to her.

"Ready?" the moving guy asks.

Leaning my arm out the window, I tap the side of the door. "Let's go make new memories."

I'm happy, and it feels damn good.

These violent delights have violent ends.

Not this time. This isn't a tragedy. We're not Romeo and Juliet. We're Rhett Masters and Chastity Griffin.

The bad boy and his good girl…who likes to get a little bad.

EPILOGUE

Pushing into her warm heat, I fuck her slow against the window where I now know I first fell in love with Chastity Griffin.

"The glass will break," she pants, and I chuckle. Lifting her, I move her to the bed. It's a twin, and covered in fluffy toys, including the giant pink bear I won at the carnival. His head has been stitched back on after she tore it off during our small breakup.

I punish her body, swallowing her moans. Her nails scrape at the flesh on my back, and it makes me pound her harder.

"Fuck me, Rhett. Fuck me harder, harder—take this pussy," she begs. She's a fucking horny little nympho. I thought I liked to fuck a lot, but she barely lets me eat, sleep, function. "I'm coming," she pants, her body tensing, her pussy walls gripping my dick like a vice. I follow her over, collapsing my sweaty skin against hers.

"You monster." She strains beneath me, giggling and squirming.

"Don't move. You'll make me hard again," I grunt.

"Mmm…really?" She wiggles.

"You're insatiable." I nibble her ear, and she giggles more. Damn, I love that sound.

"Let's eat and then fuck again." I lift myself off her and slip my dick out.

My mother was having a night in at the new house and Chasity's dad was off at some retreat or motel while the wicked stepmother is at her family's estate—which meant an empty place for us to take advantage of.

The video didn't go viral. It never went farther than Lillan's office.

We were both surprised she didn't use it to sabotage our relationship by showing Chas's dad, but there hasn't even been a squeak about it from her.

"I bought groceries." Chastity slaps my ass, hurrying past me to the bathroom.

"You'll pay for that," I shout after her, pulling off the condom and tossing it in her trashcan. I have to remember to empty that before I leave.

Pulling on some track pants, I wince when the fabric brushes over my new tattoo. It's only visible by the red raised skin, which will settle down. And then, without a black light, you won't even know it's there.

My hip adorns The Elite logo with Lust written beneath it.

The task considered complete, I was initiated fully without having to do anything or being able to refuse.

After what God did for me with Chastity, lying about him being behind the video and my insistent shit to make him join, I couldn't leave him alone in this. I doubt we will ever know who sent that video in, but it doesn't matter now. I'm an Elite Seven member, and I got the girl.

Taking the stairs two at a time, I make my way to the kitchen and open the fridge. All my favorite food stares back at me. "I love you, baby," I say aloud, even though she's upstairs showering and can't hear me.

Pulling out the makings for a sandwich, I nearly drop the food when the front door crashes open.

Grabbing a knife from the knife block, I march into the foyer and my feet skid to a stop.

Pride stands before me, wild eyed and covered in…is that…blood? Rush fills the doorway seconds later.

"What happened to you?"

"Where the fuck is she?" he growls.

"Who?" I ask manuevering my body toward the stairs to block them off. If he means my girl, he'll have to kill me to get to her. The scary fucking thing about that is he looks crazed enough to attempt it.

"Lillian," he roars, grabbing a vase from the hall table and throwing it against the wall. It shatters into a million pieces across the foyer.

The floor above me creaks.

Pride's crazy eyes follow the noise. "Where is Lillian?" he barks to Chastity, who is clutching a towel to her body, shaking from tip to toe.

"She's at her family's place. It's just us two here, man," I placate, holding up my hands, the knife still in my grip. Awkward.

"Tell me what the fuck is going on," I demand. "Whose blood is that?"

He doesn't answer, he just slams out the same way he came in.

Whose fucking blood was that?

ACKNOWLEDGEMENTS

Thank you to everyone who came on board with this project.

What an exciting ride, joining forces with my badass peers.

This title was lighter than my usual titles, but Rhett was a force and I fell head over heels in love with him.

He made me cry, laugh and swoon.

Thank you to my readers for always being open minded and taking these leaps with me.

People who make it happen.

Word Nerd Editing—As always you help iron out the worlds I create and this wouldn't be the same without you. Thank you.

Formatter: Stacey, thank you for always making allowances for my awful timing and hectic life. You're a real gem.

My proofreaders: Teresa, and Allison, thank you for always dropping everything to fit in my work. You guys are the best and I appreciate your help perfecting these stories. Kim thank you for your amazing eagle eye.

Bloggers. Thanks so much for taking a chance on his series. We couldn't do what we love without you joining us so thank you xxx

Terrie PA / Arasin's PR: Thank you for all your hard work with release and promo packets. You're awesome and always step up when I need you to.

ABOUT THE AUTHOR

My books all tend to be darker romance, edge of your seat, angst-filled reads. My advice to my readers when starting one of my titles… prepare for the unexpected.
I have always had a passion for storytelling, whether it be through lyrics or bedtime stories with my sisters growing up.

My mom would always have a book in her hand when I was young and passed on her love for reading, inspiring me to venture into writing my own. Not all love stories are made from light; some are created in darkness but are just as powerful and worth telling.

When I'm not lost in the world of characters, I love spending time with my family. I'm a mom and that comes first in my life, but when I do get down time, I love attending music concerts or reading events with my younger sister.

News Letter sign up: eepurl.com/OpJxT
Website: authorkerdukey.com
Facebook: www.facebook.com/KerDukeyauthor
Twitter: twitter.com/KerDukeyauthor

Contact me here
Ker: Kerryduke34@gmail.com
Ker's PA : terriesin@gmail.com

BOOKS BY KER

Empathy series

Empathy

Desolate

Vacant - Novella

Deadly - Novella

The Broken Series:

The Broken

The Broken Parts Of Us

The Broken Tethers That Bind Us—Novella

The Broken Forever—Novella

The Men By Numbers Series

Ten

Six

Drawn to you Duet

Drawn to you

Lines Drawn

Standalone novels:

My soul Keeper

Lost

I see you

The Beats In Rift

Devil

Co written with D. Sidebottom

The Deception series:

FaCade

Cadence

Beneath Innocence - Novella

The Lilith's Army MC series

Taking Avery

Finding Rhiannon

Coming Home TBA

Co-written with K Webster

The Pretty Little dolls series:

Pretty Stolen Dolls

Pretty Lost Dolls

Pretty New Doll

Pretty Broken Dolls

The V Games Series:

Vlad

Ven.

Vas

Joint series—
Four Fathers.

Blackstone by J.D. Hollyfield
Kingston by Dani René
Pearson by K Webster
Wheeler by Ker Dukey

Joint Series—Four Sons

Nixon by Ker Dukey
Hayden by J.D Hollyfield
Brock by Dani René
Camden by K Webster

52113831R00124

Made in the USA
Columbia, SC
27 February 2019